DEAD OF NIGHT

PAUL J. TEAGUE

ALSO BY PAUL J. TEAGUE

Two Years After

Friends Who Lie

Now You See Her

Two Years After

Friends Who Lie

Now You See Her

PART I

HUNTED

1

———

Sunday 00:23

There was a heavy thud against the bonnet of the car. Something – or someone – had emerged from the woodland, out of the fog and the darkness, onto the road in front of them.

Lucy cried out, abruptly woken from her doze.

'What the hell was that?'

It was late and, bored of chatting through the day's events with Jack, she'd been half asleep.

'Shit!' he cursed, slamming on the brakes. The car swerved onto the muddy verge. They veered too far to the left, running into a shallow ditch, the wing striking a tree. Whatever it was, it had shattered the glass of the windscreen and Jack had lost what little visibility he'd had.

'That must have been a deer. It was huge.'

Jack pulled on the handbrake and put the gear stick into neutral. As if it mattered, they weren't going anywhere.

'What lights have we got in this bloody thing?'

He scanned the control panel of the car looking for the interior light. Damn hire cars, he could never find the right switch without fiddling around for five minutes. It was cheaper to hire than it was to get the clutch changed in theirs. When he found the light switch they gasped as they saw what was splashed across the windscreen. Blood. A lot of it.

Lucy began to panic.

'Look at the mess on the window. What would do that?'

'Keep calm, Luce. I'm going out to take a look. You coming?'

'No thanks, I'll stay here. Put the headlights on full beam, you won't be able to see a thing out there. Take your phone too, you can use the torch.'

'Good idea,' said Jack, retrieving his phone from the glove compartment and opening the door.

'Christ, it's cold! Pass me my top, will you?'

Lucy reached over to grab his tracksuit top from the back seat. It was still wet. She handed it to him and then felt her ankle to see if her sprain from earlier was any better. It had been some run. They'd both done well to finish. And now it was a long drive home in the dead of night. They wanted to get back for Hamish, to be there before he woke up

'Be careful out there. It's muddy.'

'No phone signal,' Jack said as he stepped out of the car and looked at his screen. 'The car is fucked. This thing is going on a tow truck. Who knows where the nearest phone box will be, if there even is one ...'

His voice trailed off as he moved to the front of the car.

'Don't you think you should close your door?' Lucy called after him, but he didn't hear her. She tried to lean over to close it herself, but she felt a twinge of pain in her leg. A half-marathon, the first in quite some time too. Of course she was aching all over.

Jack continued to inspect the damage to the car. Lucy lowered her window as he came round to update her.

'It was big and heavy, whatever it was. There's blood on the bumper and all over the bonnet. It's made a right mess of the front. You did remove the insurance excess when you booked the car, didn't you?'

'Yes, it's fine, there's no excess. We can blame the bump in the car park on this too. It'll be less embarrassing than admitting we didn't see that low wall.'

'There's something moving over there. Please don't tell me it's still alive. I don't want to have to finish it off.'

'Is there a wheel wrench in the boot?' Lucy suggested. 'You could kill it with that. Is it cruelty to animals if you put something out of its misery?'

'Press that button next to your knee and open up the boot. I'll see if there's anything heavy in there. I can't see a bloody thing in this fog.'

Jack walked off, holding his phone out for light, for what little good it did him. Lucy gently stretched her legs, testing for pain and strains. She was stiff, but everything was moving fine. Carefully she eased herself out of the car. It was on a slope and she was getting out into a low ditch. As she took her weight on her injured ankle she became more confident realising that nothing seemed to be too badly damaged. She leant back into the footwell, fumbled around for the boot switch and heard the click as it opened. Jack was cursing several feet away. They might be needing that wrench.

Jack appeared out of the gloom. She saw the light from his phone first, then the fluorescent strips on his top. He was pale with shock, she couldn't remember when she'd seen him look like that. She immediately knew it wasn't good.

'What happened? What is it?'

Jack lurched to the side and threw up onto the muddy verge.

'It's a man,' he said, wiping his mouth with a tissue. 'We hit a man.'

'Oh, my God. Is he alive?'

'He's alive. I don't know what to do. He's barely conscious. Can you get a phone signal? Is there a first aid kit in the car?'

'Damn it, Jack. Where did he come from? We're in the middle of nowhere. How can we hit a man out here?'

'Check your phone, Luce, see if we can get some help.'

'No signal. Nothing. My battery's almost gone too. Where is he? You haven't left him in the road, have you?'

'What else could I do?'

There was a feeble moan up ahead.

They turned and walked to the front of the car.

'Jesus Christ, Jack.'

Lucy surveyed the bloody mess on the road. It was a man, forties she thought, his dark hair was greying. He wasn't dressed for the outdoors, he looked like he'd just left the office. He was wearing a shirt, no tie, and dark trousers. His right eye was blackened and bruised, his face scratched and bleeding. His leg was bent back awkwardly, exactly as he'd fallen after being struck. Bone was sticking through his torn trouser leg. His thick glasses were damaged.

This time it was Lucy who threw up. She'd seen things like that on TV, but with a real person lying there, crying with pain, it got the better of her. She wiped her face, as Jack had done, and walked back over to him to try and figure out what to do next. She struck something with her foot and knelt down to inspect it. It hadn't felt like a stone or a stick. It was the man's wallet. She picked it up, they'd need it for identification when help came.

'What shall we do?' Jack asked. 'I don't know whether we should move him or leave him here. We might do more harm than good if we carry him to the car.'

'What's your name?' Lucy asked, finding the courage to bend down and get closer to the man. He was struggling not to pass out, muttering urgently. She put her hands on his head to try to make him more comfortable, but he flinched.

'Careful, Lucy, he might have broken his spine. We can't just move him, we'll need to get some help.'

'What the fuck am I supposed to do? He's in pain, he could be dying. I wasn't the dickhead who hit him anyway!'

And there it was again. Her rage could surface at a moment's notice.

'Look, Luce, we're going to have to go for help. One of us will have to stay with him. We'll need to find the emergency triangle in the back of the car and set up some sort of cordon or warning in case another car comes along the road. There's nothing else we can do.'

She knew that he was right. And it made sense for her to stay with the man. Her ankle was not as bad as she'd thought it was, but who knew how far it was to the next village? Jack would have to go.

'You get off, try and find some help. I'll make it as safe as I can here. Put your running bib on, you'll light up better if any cars come. In fact, get mine out of the car too, it'll make us both more visible.'

In silence they put on the safety gear that they'd used during the race only hours before. Jack moved to kiss Lucy, but she was in no mood for it.

'Be as fast as you can, Jack. I don't want to be left alone here with him.'

He touched her arm and jogged off into the thickening fog. The man became agitated. At first Lucy thought it was the pain, but he was desperately trying to get her attention.

'What? What is it? What's the matter?'

She leant in closer, his voice was so weak.

'Run ...' he said, his hand reaching up to hold her arm, 'run ... for your life!'

From nowhere came headlights on full beam, a vehicle revving hard, speeding towards them. Lucy flung herself out of the way. It struck the man, spinning his body with the force of the blow. Lucy gasped.

'Jack!' she screamed, but he didn't hear her, he was too far along the road.

The vehicle stopped beyond their own car, and she heard the change of gears as it started to reverse. The passenger door opened. She saw a hand, it was holding something. It was a gun. She saw the light as it fired, the bullet hitting the injured man's head, its impact spattering her with blood.

Lucy watched as the shooter fired a second bullet into the body and then levelled up his weapon to aim at her. She'd seen all she needed to. Still clutching the wallet, she turned towards the trees and did exactly what the man had told her to do.

She was running for her life.

2

———

Three Weeks Before The Race

'How are we doing for time?' Lucy asked, breathless and in need of more practice runs like this before the main event took place.

'You're doing well, just over 105 minutes, we'll finish in under two hours.'

Jack's phone beeped. He kept it safely in an armband while he was running.

'Do you have to wear that bloody thing all the time? Can't we just go for a quiet run?'

'It's how I motivate myself,' Jack replied.

They'd had this conversation a hundred times. Here it was again.

'It's called accountability, you should try it sometime. It pushes me on if I know somebody's doing better than me with their times. Clive, for instance. That bastard cut five minutes off his time last week. I'm not allowing that.

Besides, I like reading all the comments on Facebook when I've finished. And it helps me connect with other runners—'

He stopped mid-sentence. He was justifying himself too much. She'd never get it. Lucy didn't like social media and would never dream of sharing what was going on in her life so publicly. He glanced over towards his wife. She was struggling to keep up with him. He wanted to run ahead and whip Clive's arse, but he thought he'd better keep pace with her. She'd done well to get back into shape so fast, he knew how difficult it had been for her. They needed this. It was important that they still did this together.

Her cleavage was beginning to glisten with sweat. It always turned him on when he saw her like that. Before Hamish, he'd have burned up all his excess energy as soon as they got home. These days she dived straight into the shower to get freshened up.

'Fifteen minutes max,' he encouraged. 'Do you want to try for a final burst?'

'No, let's not push for time. How about we slow down a bit and talk. We'll be back soon and Maxine will need to get home. She's leaving for uni in a couple of months, she won't be available for much longer.'

Good old Maxine. She'd been a godsend, particularly when Lucy had been really down. Things couldn't have been much worse for them. Fancy losing your job when your wife's just gone on maternity leave and your first child is due in less than a month.

Maxine was one of those rare eighteen-year-olds who looked like she still inhabited a more innocent world where the Famous Five wouldn't be out of place. She lived in the social housing in the next village, she'd had a stable, but uneventful, upbringing and the banality of rural life was driving her crazy.

Maxine was getting out of there. She'd almost missed her chance, dropping a grade in her A-levels and being rejected for the summer intake. Thanks to her cutting-edge university, she was able to get a place on a second-semester start course, but only after a period of additional and intensive study. She'd made it, albeit a little later than her school chums. Nothing was going to distract her from her studies or mess up her future, she wanted this more than anything.

She was perfect for Hamish, who seemed to sense his mother's unhappiness the moment he entered the world. They were constantly at odds with each other. Jack hated himself for it, but sometimes he thought couldn't have picked a better time to have to be away from home so much, working on a contract.

It was as if she'd read his mind.

'What time do you have to leave this evening?'

He was getting angry again, and he always ran faster when he was wound up. Lucy was short of breath. He'd need to cool off, she wouldn't thank him for wearing her out. He slowed a little, he could see Lucy was tiring. Her face was reddening now, and that wasn't so sexy.

'I have to catch the train at six. You know I'd rather be at home with you and Hamie. I don't have a choice, we need the money. Until you can get a job—'

'And how the fuck am I going to get a job living in that bloody house!'

Her outburst was ferocious. She was always difficult on Sundays, it meant another week on her own with Hamish.

She stopped running, bent over and caught her breath. Jack kept his cursing to himself. That bugger Clive would get to keep his time record for another week. He knew they needed to run together like this, but she slowed him down. And they had met at the running club, after all. It's what they had in common at the beginning. Now it seemed to be all they had in common. And the baby, of course.

'I'm sorry, Jack, I didn't mean it. I feel so isolated in that damn house. It seemed such a good idea when it was only us, but now ... well, you know what I think.'

Jack ran on the spot for a few seconds, then realised that Lucy was done. They'd be walking for the rest of the way. Clive would take the piss when his GPS tracker recorded his route and timings.

'Had to stop for a rest, old man?' he'd jeer. The bastard, he knew how it was with Lucy. They'd had long enough to discuss it on the train to Aberdeen.

'If I can keep this contract going for another few months, I'll be able to get rid of that ridiculous sports car. What were we thinking of, buying a two-seater? I suppose it was sensible enough before Hamish came along. Anyway, the contract is still month-to-month. We'll be in shit street if we lose the house. When I make up the missed payments, I promise we'll get a decent family car. But it still might go tits up. If it does, we'll be struggling again.'

It was a delightful cocktail of rural isolation, closed bus routes, no money and marital tension. Truth be told, Jack was finding it easier to step on that train every Sunday evening and return on the Thursday evening. They'd cut him some slack, let him work from home on Fridays. But they didn't pay his rail fares or hotel bills, so he was making very little out of the deal by the time everything was paid.

He saw the bright red *For Sale* sign in the distance. It was easy enough to spot, for Christ's sake. Why was no bugger buying it? It was probably to do with the closed village shop and the threatened community school. Even if they stayed, there was no way Hamish would ever get to attend the local school. It had just under fifty pupils. What's idyllic to parents is an obvious cost-saving target for councillors. Its days had to be numbered.

'I'll see if they'll let me work from home on Thursdays too, but it's difficult, they need me there in the office. I have to be there in person or they can't access the software. I'll try though.'

Lucy was recovering her breath. She too had seen the *For Sale* sign and wanted to avoid the house a little longer. She knew that Jack suspected her motives when she offered to run Maxine back home in the car. It was another twenty minutes away from that albatross of a house. And, yes, away from the baby. She could barely admit it to herself, let alone Jack or the health visitor, but she was struggling with Hamish. The runs gave her headspace. Sometimes she wanted to escape. From everything. Jack too. They'd been in love once, but it was slipping away from them. And if she and Jack split up, she couldn't face being left on her own with Hamish. She hated herself. She'd never had depression before becoming a mother. She despised herself and what it had done to her.

'We'd better get back,' Jack said. 'Maxine will want another fiver if we break into a new hour. Race you?'

There was a time when she'd have smiled at him, her face glowing with health and vigour, and they'd slam their hands on the front door to show who'd got there first. He always let her win. She knew it, but he'd get his reward, either on the kitchen table, on the rug in the sitting room, sometimes in the bedroom, and even in the garden at the back of the house once. That passion seemed a long way off now.

'You run, I'll walk back. I'm tired. I'll not be long.'

Jack looked at Lucy and studied her face for a moment. He wasn't sure how long they'd got left. He could see she was close to breaking point, but what could he do? If they lost the house, things would only get worse. It had seemed so idyllic living in a big house in the country before the company went bust. Now he just felt like an idiot.

Jack picked up his pace, sprinting towards the house at great speed, craving the shot of adrenalin that it would give him. Maxine had spotted them coming along the road. She was obviously jittery, wanting to return home and get on with her studies. She was taking university very seriously, before it had even begun. What would they do when Maxine left? She'd been a great find. And there was Hamish, calm, happy and relaxed. He grew fidgety as Lucy walked up the garden path.

'Hey Maxine!' she waved, as if she hadn't a care in the world.

'Good run?' Maxine asked, getting ready to hold out Hamish so that she could take the baby. Lucy didn't respond to the cue. Maxine held him tightly, giving him a little squeeze. He began to gurgle happily again.

'How about you take Hamie and I run Maxine back home?' Lucy suggested. Seconds later she was inside the house and had come out with the car keys.

Jack moved close to Maxine and took the baby from her. He sat Hamish on his hip as he stepped inside the door and fumbled through his wallet for a couple of notes.

'Ten pounds, Maxine, is that right?' Jack asked, holding out two fivers.

'Actually, Mr Dawson, we're ten minutes into a new hour. We did agree ...'

'Yes, of course, Maxine, no problem,' he replied, changing one of the notes for a tenner.

'Watch the clutch, Lucy,' he called over as his wife got into the car. 'It's slipping a bit at the moment, we'll need to get it looked at – as soon as we can afford it.'

3

———

Three Weeks Before The Race

'You creaky old bastard, you're getting past it, you know.'

Jack wouldn't really describe Clive as a friend. He was more of a necessity. He'd bailed Jack out of a deep hole and got him the contract. He owed him, but that didn't mean he had to like him.

The whistle sounded on the platform and the train began to move. He daren't tell Lucy that they were travelling First Class to Aberdeen. The first time he'd met Clive on the platform to travel up there, he'd assumed that Jack would be sitting in First, like him. Jack had kept his cool, pretended to go off to the buffet, and sorted out an upgrade with the conductor before he reached them with his ticket checking. After that, Jack booked tickets online, trying to get them in advance to make them as cheap as he could. Clive was not the type of person he wanted to admit his money problems to.

'How's Sophie?' he asked, changing the subject.

'Oh, you know, can't get enough of me, wants to jump my bones all the time. I have to travel to Aberdeen to get a break from her. A man can only take so much!'

Jack didn't like the way Clive talked about Sophie. He'd only met her once in passing. It was when the company was flourishing and Clive was a much-valued contractor. She seemed nice, not the sort of woman who'd put with Clive. He was all testosterone and bravado.

'Are you doing the run then? With Lucy? Or are you too chicken?'

Everything was competitive with Clive: work, running, sex with your wife. He could never let anything go. And it irked Jack all the more because he was succeeding at none of them.

'Yes, I think we will actually. Lucy's been doing well with picking it up again. I don't envy her, she's been out of it for quite some time. I think it's done her good though—'

He stopped short. There was no way he was talking to Clive about his marital issues. It would be all over the office.

'Sophie loves kids, she would come over and look after your little lad for the weekend. In fact, we could both come over, give you a weekend off. It might stop her trying to get me to fuck her so much. She's desperate for a baby, you know. I can't stand them – no offence.'

'None taken,' Jack replied, though he suspected it wouldn't have made much difference if he had been put out by the comment.

'How tough is the terrain? It's Scottish lowlands, isn't it – not one of those river and hills runs? Lucy won't want anything too serious, it must be well over a year since we did anything competitive.'

'Yeah, yeah, it's all fine. Lovely countryside and all that. And I'd love to meet Lucy, see how hot she is in her Lycra.

My missus only goes to the gym when I'm away so I never get to see her in her gym gear. No offence like. About Lucy.'

Jack wanted to punch the idiot, but he gave a non-committal smile. He needed Clive. As Jack's company had been going to the dogs, Clive had moved on to bigger and better things. He was now working for the Pharmexus Corporation, a giant pharmaceuticals company with its UK base in Aberdeen of all places. Cold and isolated, it was the perfect place to work and spend no money. And it was a devil of a journey by train too.

Jack didn't know much about the pharmaceuticals industry other than that Clive was in a much more lucrative part of the business than he was. Jack was on the tech side, running software simulations for some project or another. He was comfortable with the code and programming, he didn't pretend to understand the other stuff. He'd worked out that a lot of people in suits were getting excited. It was something to do with Alzheimer's disease research and it seemed to be going very well. All Jack knew for sure was that once he'd delivered the modelling infrastructure for them, he'd be out on his arse again.

It was Clive who'd got him into the GPS tracking. He liked it, he admired the engineering and technical achievement. He could go out on a run, wear his tracker, and all the time his route, his speed, his heartbeat – everything was there on social media for his running buddies to view. Clive even knew he'd stopped off for a piss in the hedge once. He could tell by the reduced heart rate and duration of the change.

'Stopped for a pee last night?' he'd laughed. 'I could tell. Your heart rate dipped for about a minute. You were away so fast you can barely have had time to shake!'

There was always a wisecrack with Clive. And it was

usually at somebody else's expense. Jack tried to keep the conversation on neutral ground. Aberdeen seemed an awfully long way away.

'Why don't you and Sophie come around for dinner one night in the next fortnight? It would be good to get to know Sophie better and if you're serious about looking after Hamish it would be timely for you to meet him before you sign on the dotted line. I'll speak to Lucy when we get to the hotel this evening. What do you think?'

'I like it, mate, but don't blame me if that wife of yours decides to leave you after she gets her eyes on Clivey. I may be forty now, but I'm still ripped and I've got buns of steel.'

Clive started to scroll through his Facebook feed.

'That bastard Simon beat my thirteen-mile record. By seven minutes too. Shit, I can't let that one stand. He's far too fit for my liking. And he's fifty-six. Imagine being like that at his age. Bastard!'

Jack had had enough of Clive's nonsense. They still had a couple of hours to go until they reached their destination, so Jack decided to call Lucy about the meal. And the run. He knew she'd say yes. Anything to get away from Hamish. What could he do? She'd had post-natal depression. Her mum was dead and his parents were too old to help. They just had to get on with it.

He was as certain as he could be that she was okay now. He'd had a quiet word with the health visitor, checking that Hamish was safe to be left with her. It wasn't like that, or at least he didn't think so. She'd been so down after he was born. They'd never really bonded. Hamish seemed to sense how uneasy his mum was around him. And poor Lucy, she associated the baby with a really shit time in her life. It didn't help that he was out hunting for work when it happened too.

'Luce? Hey, it's Jack. Yes, everything's fine. I wanted to run something by you before the phone signal dies. You know that run we talked about? Yes, the one at Loch Lomond. Are you up for it still?'

For a moment, Jack thought it was going to be a no. He heard Hamish crying in the background. Lucy sighed then gave her answer.

'What about a babysitter? Who'll look after the baby? Hamish. Who'll look after Hamish?'

'Luce—' Jack said.

'I'm trying, Jack, honestly I am. We're getting there. I'm trying.'

'Clive says he and Sophie will stay and look after Hamie. I invited them over for dinner to meet you both. Are you up for it? We'd get some time away on our own. It would be good for us.'

Hamish was growing increasingly unhappy, his whimpering was about to turn into a full-blown cry. Lucy sighed again.

'Okay, let's do it,' she said. 'You're right, it will be good to do this together. We can travel up the night before then drive back afterwards. Will Clive and Sophie stay over?'

'Yes, he seems pretty keen for me to do the run,' Jack said, trying to conceal his joy at her decision. 'I think he'd do an overnighter. Sophie loves babies, apparently. Clive, not so much.'

'Okay, let's do it! I'll book online after I put Hamish to bed. You mean the half-marathon though, right? I'm not ready for more than that at the moment.'

'Yes, great, the thirteen-miler. It'll be fun. Like old times.'

Jack finished the call and returned to his seat opposite Clive.

'We're on!' he said, smiling. 'It's a goer. And you and

Sophie can come around for dinner too. Is this Saturday okay?'

Clive nodded. They'd all get to know each other and in three weeks' time, he and Lucy would run the Loch Lomond half-marathon. It would give her something to aim for and provide a break from Hamish. He didn't know then that he'd just committed them both to the worst night of their lives.

4

———

Sunday 00:37

Jack was surprised at how much energy he had. He always had trouble getting warmed up when it was so cold, but now, jogging in that damp, oppressive fog, he felt as if he could run forever.

Would the man die? He was badly injured, dazed and delirious. And there was something about him that bothered Jack. He churned over his own culpability. Was it dangerous driving? Careless driving perhaps? They were in the middle of nowhere, **it was after midnight**, who would expect a man to walk into the path of a car? Even if he'd needed to flag them down for help, he still should have stood at the side of the road. Only a fool would stand in front of a vehicle on a night like that.

The police would need to get involved, there'd be an insurance claim, an investigation and a lot of paperwork. But Jack was no weasel. He'd hit somebody. However blame was apportioned, whoever got the finger pointed at them, his first priority was to do what he could to help this man.

Jack sped up slightly. Would there even be a phone box in the next village? He pulled out his mobile and looked at the screen. One bar flickered on and off. If he was lucky, the signal would get better as he neared civilisation, it wasn't steady enough yet to make a call.

Jack tried to visualise the man's face as he ran along the side of the road dodging muddy puddles and potholes. It had been bruised and bloodied. He wore glasses, but they'd been broken in the accident, hanging off his ear by one of the arms. It was a daft thing to do, but it was the first thing that Jack had done when he stepped up to him as he lay in the road. He'd removed his broken glasses. They were thick and heavy, that's what he'd noticed, thicker than Jack had ever seen anyone else wearing. Except one other man, a contractor he'd met at work.

Yes, that was what had been bothering Jack. Could it be the same person? Could the man he'd hit really be employed in the same workplace? He'd never spoken to the contractor directly but he had clocked him as he moved around the building. If he'd been asked to describe him he'd have said 'dark, greying hair with heavy, thick glasses'. He tried to picture the man who'd been lying in the road. He was the same sort of age, same build. What was his hair colour? Jack couldn't remember, he'd had to rush off to vomit at that point. No, of course it couldn't be him. They were miles from Aberdeen, that would be ridiculous.

He jogged on at a steady pace. He shuddered. Suddenly a loud noise disturbed the silence. A gunshot. Then another one. Who could be shooting at this time of night? A game-keeper? He thought not.

The noise was definitely coming from behind him. He

stopped and listened. There was one final shot. Jack stood panting at the side of the road. He'd left Lucy on her own with no phone signal and only an injured man for company. He turned back, running faster than he had before. As he rounded a bend in the road, he saw the bright headlights of a vehicle ahead. Perhaps a car had stopped to help Lucy and would raise the alarm for them.

As Jack neared the scene of the accident, a flash of flames roared up into the night sky. He gasped. The hire car was on fire. Had they ruptured the fuel tank when they went into the ditch? Surely not. Those things were supposed to be impregnable.

He felt a dark sense of dread. He hadn't seen it before, but this was no random event. A man running into the road in the dead of night. The sounds of gunshot. A burning car. He had to get to Lucy.

He ducked off the road and began to make his way through the trees to the scene of the accident. Two Mercedes crew vans were parked on the opposite verge and a group of men all carrying handguns were standing nearby, silhouetted against the flames from the burning vehicle. Jack counted eight of them. They'd come dressed for the occasion wearing boots and combat jackets. This was no late-night poaching trip.

He surveyed the scene, looking for Lucy, desperately trying to make out her figure among the shapes in front of him. Nothing. She wasn't there. Had she run? A wave of panic engulfed him. What the fuck was going on?

He looked at the burning car. There was a body sitting at the wheel, it was on fire. Lucy! Surely that wasn't Lucy. Panic turned to rage as Jack considered the possibility that it might be his wife burning in that car.

He'd have to risk being seen in the light of the flames.

He had his hi-viz bib on, that would give the game away. Jack took it off and threw it into the trees. He thought about doing the same with his tracksuit top, but it was cold out there, so instead he turned it inside out.

He crept through the trees towards the burning car. The heat was intense, the metal of the bodywork expanding and creaking noisily. He couldn't see clearly enough. He would have to go into the road to get a proper look. He had to know if it was Lucy in there. The men seemed to be studying a map, planning their next move.

Watching them like a hawk, Jack quietly made his way into the road. He was lit up entirely by the flames. If they turned around, there was no way he could stay hidden. He had to risk it. He had to get a good look at the burning body. It was charred already but he could see enough to know that it wasn't Lucy. It was a man, it must be the man they'd struck earlier.

He'd been spotted. First he noticed the hum of the voices changing, and then, out of the corner of his eyes, an urgent movement – focused on him.

Suddenly there was a whoosh of petrol flames as the fuel tank exploded and the entire area was engulfed in a searing heat. Jack was pushed back into the middle of the road. He stumbled, struggling to keep his footing.

He heard a shout from the approaching figures.

'It's him! Don't lose him!'

Jack did the only thing open to him. He ran as fast as he could into the dark, wet woodland.

5

Two Weeks Before The Race

Lucy placed the small teddy bear at the side of the headstone and repositioned the tiny posy of flowers for the fifth time. Behind her, Hamish was stirring in the pram.

She wished that Jack was there. His presence would give her strength. She couldn't stop the tears. When would the pain subside? It still hurt so bad, even after six months. She craved the rawness to end.

Helen. She had a name, even if she'd barely spent a day alive. They'd chatted for hours about having twins with names that began with the same letter. Was it a bit naff? Well, they wouldn't get to use the names together now.

Jack never came to the cemetery. He was always so tired when he got back from Aberdeen. They barely had time to catch their breath. They were dealing with a birth and a death. The child that survived still needed their attention, but Lucy was finding it hard to love him. How could she feel like that? What kind of mother was she?

She dared not share her thoughts with the health visitor. In fact, she wished the woman would get out of their lives. Lucy felt so watched all of the time. She worried that any admission of resentment towards Hamish would get her banished to a psychiatric ward at the drop of a hat. As for Jack, he was too busy trying to keep it all going. Would it matter if everything collapsed? Lucy wondered if they might be happier.

She wiped the tears from her face. There was a movement behind her. Someone was approaching cautiously, not wishing to invade her private moment but clearly wanting to speak. Lucy turned around. A middle-aged woman in a long dark coat and leather boots was peering into the pram at Hamish. Her black hair was threaded with grey.

'They're lovely at that age, aren't they? They look so peaceful when they're asleep.'

Lucy didn't want to talk about babies, but the woman persisted. She was intent on striking up a conversation. Lucy usually had the cemetery to herself during the week. She would stand in front of the grave silently weeping, recalling how she'd held Helen, her firstborn, and how elated they had been. She'd watched Jack holding Hamish, born eighteen minutes after his sister and demanding all the attention already. It was as if he'd stolen her air, as if he'd denied his own sister's chance of life.

'I'm so sorry for your loss. It must be very difficult—'

'Do I know you?' Lucy snapped.

The woman looked at her. She didn't seem offended by Lucy's outburst. She seemed tough, as if she'd dealt with much worse.

'I'm so sorry!' Lucy burst into tears. 'It's just ... I can't really talk about it, it's still so hard.'

The woman put her arm around Lucy, holding her,

letting her cry without inhibition, it felt good. She remained silent, waiting for Lucy to compose herself again.

'Shall we sit on the bench?' the woman asked, sensing that Lucy had calmed down.

'I'm sorry if I upset you. I assumed you were at a parent's or grandparent's grave when I walked over to you. I hadn't thought that it might have been your child. I'm sorry.'

'It's fine, life has to go on. People behave as if they're walking on eggshells around me. I'm tired of talking about it. All I want is for the pain to go away, or at least subside a bit. Will it always be like this?'

The woman studied Lucy's face. She seemed sympathetic, but there was no real warmth there.

'I can't even begin to think what you must be going through. And on your own too—'

'Oh no, the father is still with me. Jack, I mean. We're together still. He's at work. He works away from home. In Aberdeen.'

The woman nodded.

'Do you live far from here?' she asked. 'I have my car parked outside. I'm happy to run you home if that would help?'

It was growing dark already. Damn winter, stealing the daylight so fast. Lucy must have been there for well over an hour, she'd been lost in her thoughts.

'I live about a mile away, maybe a little more than that. I don't want to trouble you ...'

'It's no trouble at all. It's getting cold, you don't want the little one to be out too long in weather like this.'

Lucy thought little of it then, but she did notice. The woman's English was excellent, but she detected a hint of German in the way she spoke.

'A lift would be great, thank you.'

She walked over to the pram, took off the brake, and they started to walk towards the gate.

'Who do you come to visit here?' Lucy asked. 'I haven't seen you around, have I? Are you local?'

The woman seemed caught off her guard at that.

'No, no, I'm not local, not nowadays anyway. My mother is buried here. I come to visit her whenever I find myself in the county. I don't have much cause to be here these days, I feel guilty that I don't get to see her as often as I should.'

They neared the cemetery entrance, and Lucy discarded the packaging from the teddy bear that she'd placed on Helen's grave.

'What's her surname?' Lucy asked. 'I might know of her. We've been here a while now, we're slowly getting to know more about the place.'

Again the woman floundered a little, then quickly recovered.

'That's my mum over there. Near the entrance. Always had to be the centre of attention!' She gave a short laugh. Lucy looked at the gravestone. Elsie Martin. Died two years previously.

'Here we are. How do you want to carry the baby? If you put the pram top in the rear seat belts, he'll be safe enough for a mile. I'll drive slowly.'

Lucy fastened Hamish securely on the back seat. She made doubly sure that he was safe. It reminded her of that thing Jack always said about cats: 'I don't particularly like them but I'd never hurt one'. Is that how she felt about her son? She hated herself for it.

The drive to the house only took a few minutes. It would have taken Lucy half an hour to walk it with the pram. She'd been careless letting the time slip away from her like that.

'Here you are, what a delightful house. And so remote too. I bet it's lovely and quiet here.'

'It's noisier than the city,' Lucy replied, 'particularly in the summer when all the wildlife is out and about. What with wood pigeons, pheasants and owls, it can be a right cacophony sometimes.'

'You prefer to be somewhere busier then?'

'Yes, this place can't sell soon enough as far as I'm concerned!'

Lucy stepped out of the car and awkwardly lifted the carrycot off the back seat and clipped it back onto the pram frame.

'Thanks so much for the lift,' she said, giving a wave.

She walked up to the house, opened the front door and turned on the lights. She noticed as she took off her coat, switched on the kettle and attended to a crying Hamish, that the woman was parked out on the road for some time. She seemed to be studying something, a map perhaps. Every now and then Lucy would glance out of the window to see if she was still there. After ten minutes, she was on her way.

What an unusual encounter. There was nothing particularly strange or threatening about the woman, but it did all seem a bit odd. She never saw anybody at the cemetery. And the woman had been mistaken when she'd indicated her mother's grave.

Elsie Martin was a well-known villager, even to newcomers like Lucy. She was quite a character, and was often to be seen riding about on a rusty old bicycle. She'd been the village teacher and lived in the Old School House before it had been sold off, given a makeover, and become somebody else's expensive home. She'd been the last teacher to live there before she moved into her retirement bungalow.

Lucy hadn't known her that well, but there was one thing about Elsie Martin that she definitely knew. Elsie had never married and never had any children. She'd lived in the village as a single woman for almost all of her life.

6

———————

Two Weeks Before The Race

Jack stared out of the office window thinking about Lucy. He'd made a habit of visiting the cemetery alone on his drive to the station or, if he was back early enough, on his way home. He hadn't got a clue if he was doing the right thing, but he didn't want to encourage her to dwell on their loss.

It wasn't doing any good, mind you; the flowers were always fresh when he went and the grave perfectly tended. The turfs hadn't even fully taken yet, you could still clearly see the mosaic of squares through the slowly thickening grass.

When had they stopped talking about Helen? They mentioned her, of course, but when had the well run dry with new things to say? He was spent. He had nothing else to offer. They would somehow have to learn to live with it and go about their lives. Maybe the pain would subside one day. It was too early to tell. But for the time being, work was an excellent distraction.

It had been the lowest point in his life walking with that tiny coffin to the grave. At least they'd got to hold her, even if it was only for a few precious minutes. They'd got a photograph too, he'd often open it up and look at it on his phone.

The thing that was supposed to unite them, to bind them together forever, was the thing that was now driving them apart. They lived in a daze of Jack working away, trying to make enough money to stop the house being taken away from them, and caring for the child who survived. He knew that Lucy was struggling, it ate at him every hour of the day, but he had run out of things to offer. He simply didn't know what to do to help her anymore. And if their relationship didn't survive, it would be a second death to grieve over.

Clive walked into the room. He was on his way to lunch.

'Need anything from town?' he asked. 'I fancy that new sushi bar that opened last week. I'll bring you something back if you're busy?'

As Clive shuffled from foot to foot, Jack said, 'I'm cutting out lunches until we get this run out of the way. I'm carrying more weight than I should. I feel quite heavy when I start to jog.'

A man with dark hair and thick glasses popped his head around the door.

'Still okay for two o'clock?' he asked Clive, nodding to acknowledge Jack.

'Yep, yes, I'll be done by then,' Clive answered and the man was on his way.

Jack raised his eyebrows, he hadn't met this person before, though he'd seen him around the building.

'That was Matt Rackham. You might not know him, but he needs you. You're the geek who creates the code that lets him run his simulations. Without you, he'd be a pharmacist working behind the counter in Boots.'

'Oh, so he's Matt. I've heard about him, but never met him before. Looks like a clever chap. Why do they keep us all apart like that? I couldn't even tell you where his office is.'

'That's how they like it. This pharmaceuticals stuff is big bucks. Imagine you invented Viagra and some Chinese Arthur Daley stole the recipe and started selling it a zillion pounds cheaper. You'd be in shit street. You invest all that money in research and testing, and some bugger steals your secret and undercuts you in the market place. It all has to stay separate. The right hand mustn't know what the left hand is doing.'

'Wow! I'd never thought about it like that. I sit up here banging out the code and I've no idea how they're using it. I just pass it on to the next department.'

'So what bollocks were you saying about not eating lunch? Are you serious? You can do that run backwards, and in your sleep.'

'Who's that woman talking to Matt now? Is something going on here today? There seem to be a lot of unfamiliar faces around the place.'

Clive peered out of the glass once again.

'Don't know her,' he replied, awkwardly. 'Never seen her. Looks like a snooty old cow to me. I like those leather boots though. Might get Soph some of those. They'd look good on a woman twenty years younger.'

Jack let it slide again. He only had to tolerate Clive long enough to find something that paid as well closer to home. Then he could tell him to fuck off and stick his sexist and offensive comments.

'So, last chance. Sushi in a tub or starvation? Which one is it going to be?'

'Starvation,' Jack replied. 'Sorry, but if I'm going to get Lucy through this run, I need to be in the best shape that I can be so I can support her. I think it will be good for her if she achieves this. She'll feel like she's got a bit of her old life back.'

'If you ask me, you just need to jump back on the horse and get riding again, if you know what I mean?'

Jack knew exactly what Clive meant and he wanted to punch him in the face for it. Again, he held steady. He'd have to find another job soon. He was in danger of killing Clive. Essentially, there was nothing wrong with him. He wasn't a bad man, but he couldn't stop shit coming out of his mouth. He didn't seem to realise how much offence he was causing with his glib comments.

'Anyhow, your loss,' Clive finished, waving and exiting Jack's office. Jack completed a couple of lines of code, ran it and checked it in a simulation environment, then marked it as finished in the task tracker used by the company. He was doing some good work, he hoped that they appreciated his skills.

He checked his phone. Nothing from Lucy. All was quiet. He checked his Facebook account to give Clive plenty of time to get away from the building. More comments on his last run. It was amazing how many people saw the routes when they were posted live to his feed. He loved a bit of technology. Not much good if you're trying to sneak an affair behind somebody's back though.

Jack had lied to Clive. He was eating lunch, but it wouldn't be sushi. And he'd be eating it alone. He got up, walked to his window and peered out over the car park. There was Clive. By the time Jack set off he'd be well ahead. To be certain, he'd pop into the gents on the way out. Clive would have a five-minute head start on him.

As Jack was washing his hands, the woman he'd been surveying earlier came out of another cubicle. Jack hated unisex toilets, he didn't want to share private moments with members of the opposite sex. There were certain things that he didn't want to hear his female colleagues doing.

'You're Mr Dawson, aren't you?'

It took him by surprise. He'd never seen this woman in his life before.

'Yes, Jack Dawson. I'm in simulations. A geek.'

'Yes, I know all about you,' she replied. 'Your work is of crucial importance to the company.'

This struck Jack as strange.

'Do you work for Pharmexus?' he asked. For all he knew, she owned it. He'd long ago learned never to make judgements about people based on their appearance.

'No, just visiting. Call it reconnaissance. We're supposed to have an open and trusting relationship with you, but I can't get near this new drug that you're working on. Must be something very special. They've cured the common cold or something like that! Either way, I can't get a sniff of it. I'm Anna, by the way. Pleased to meet you.'

Jack recalled Clive's earlier Viagra comment.

'So you work for another pharmaceuticals company?'

'Yes, we're based in Germany. We're collaborating on a stem cell research project. It's going well, but I'd love to know what you're onto here. There's a buzz about the place. I can smell it. There's a breakthrough in the air.'

'I'm only a tech guy. No secrets here. Only an opportunity to make your eyes glaze over with some coding talk.'

Jack dried his hands on a paper towel and threw it into the bin.

'Nice to meet you, anyway,' Jack said, deciding not to

extend his hand. It never seemed the right thing to do in the toilets.

At the time it was nothing out of the ordinary, another casual encounter with somebody at work. He thought little of it, he forgot the woman the moment he walked out of the washroom. But the next time he saw her, she would be in his house, threatening the lives of his family.

7

Sunday 00:51

Jack ran through the trees, cracking fallen twigs with his feet and scratching his face with brambles and branches. He was moving faster than he ever had in any race.

He saw that everything was linked, but he couldn't understand how. The man they hit must have been running, fleeing for his life, just as he was now. Had he been dead when they set fire to the car? He hoped to God he was. And where was Lucy? She had to be somewhere in the woods, or had they got her in one of the vehicles? He hadn't even thought of that.

If she'd run into the woods, she would have taken the same side of the road as he had. The ditch on the opposite side was deeper and had water in it. It was more of a stream than a ditch and was not the easiest way to make a quick exit.

He thought about the hire car. He almost laughed aloud when he thought how they'd discussed their insurance cover earlier. It was all a bit immaterial now. The charred remains of a body might be the more pressing issue.

The fog was lifting slightly and Jack stopped in a clearing to get his bearings. He could hear voices and see torches flashing behind him. He'd got a good lead on his pursuers and he took a moment to get his breath back. They had guns, and he had every belief that they intended using them.

But why? Had he and Lucy stumbled across something that they shouldn't have seen? A drugs deal? Perhaps it was simply a case of wrong time, wrong place? He didn't know, but this was no half-hearted search. It had the urgency of a manhunt.

Jack had to plan, he couldn't just run. He counted the torch beams, there were at least five of them. He couldn't defend himself against that many men. There was something military about them – the way they dressed and the way they handled themselves. Had he and Lucy stumbled on a covert armed operation?

There was a crunch as a twig snapped up ahead. It was only a few metres away from him. Urgently he searched the dark, trying to see what it was. It was a deer, a beautiful creature, completely unaware that Jack was there. He froze. The men had gone quiet in the distance, maybe he'd shaken them off. Then a sudden flash, the sound of gunfire, the splash of blood across his face. Was this what it was like to be shot? The deer crashed to the ground. It hadn't moved at first. It was as if for a moment the animal had been as shocked by the gun as he was.

Jack stepped back, treading carefully. He took refuge behind a large tree. A cheer went up from the gang of men in the distance. They were making no attempt to conceal their whereabouts. It was so remote out there that there was no chance some householder would hear the shots and alert the police.

Jack watched as the lights began to advance towards him more quickly now. His pursuers certainly knew how to shoot. He looked at the beautiful creature, its neck blown apart by the impact of the shot. They were talking loudly and laughing, congratulating whoever had pulled the trigger.

They were close enough for Jack to hear their breathing as they gathered around the carcass to survey their prey. Would he be next? They prodded the animal with their boots, as if looking for signs of life. It was dead alright, there was no chance it could have survived.

'He can't be far from here!' one of them said. 'The river runs just over there, we'll hear it soon. There's no way he's crossing that, too much rain recently. We'll follow him downhill, and catch him when he gets to it.'

There was no mention of Lucy. It was him they were after. And there was a river, a block to him continuing through the woods. He'd be herded along the riverbank. If he headed uphill, back to the road, he'd have to run for miles to reach the next village. These men knew the area. His only option was to head downhill and somehow reach the village cross country, or at the very least somewhere where his phone would find a signal if he was going to stand any chance of getting help.

Where was Lucy? They hadn't mentioned her, it was him they were after. Was she in one of the cars already?

He held his breath as one of the men began to relieve himself against the tree. The puddle of steaming urine trickled along the woodland floor and touched the sole of his trainer. He was inches away from the man, his shotgun propped against the tree trunk.

Jack was completely still. He considered snatching the gun. He thought back to when he was a teenager and he and a friend who had lived on a farm had shot at empty paint pots out in the fields. A shotgun would have two barrels, so a maximum of two shots, depending on what kind of gun it was. The way the neck of the deer had been blown away suggested that he'd shot from both barrels, so maybe he hadn't even reloaded yet. He decided not to make a grab for the weapon – he'd give himself away and it might well be empty. The others had handguns, who knew how many shots they could fire?

The man zipped up, picked up the gun and headed back to the small clearing.

'Must be a cold night. Looking a bit small there, Blake!'

It was a woman's voice. He hadn't expected that. One of them was a woman.

Jack watched Blake's hand move to the knife he kept in a sheath attached to his belt. For a moment he thought he was going to take it out and gut her. There was a pause, then he laughed.

'You should know, Rosa. You've seen enough cocks in your life!'

It was forced, but it eased the tension. His hand moved away from the large hunting knife to his cartridges. He reloaded the shotgun. Jack watched, assessing them, trying to calculate if he could outrun them, he certainly wouldn't be able to fight them.

They were big and strong, violent too, he'd seen that already. Even Rosa looked formidable. Jack was wiry and athletic – sure, he could run, but he was defenceless in every other way. His only chance of getting away was fitness and cunning, these guys looked tough but they were too heavy to keep up with him in a test of speed.

As he heard them discussing how they would scour the woods, Jack considered stepping out from behind the tree which had done such an effective job in shielding him. Could he talk his way out of this situation? Leaning against the trunk, his breathing gradually returned to normal and for a few seconds it felt like the right thing to do. He didn't know if he was up to this dangerous game of cat and mouse.

Then, as had happened with the deer minutes earlier, there was the snap of a twig in the distance. Immediately the men jumped into action. Jack saw how well they worked in a team. They had to be military.

The torches pointed in the direction of the sound.

'It's him!'

'Stick to the plan, Arne! You work back uphill to cut him off and make sure he heads down towards the river. The rest of you, fan out wide and diagonally, keep him to the water's edge.'

For a moment, Jack thought the game was up, that they'd spotted him behind the tree. But the torches were shining ahead into the distance. Then he saw it, a glimpse of a fluorescent strip reflecting in the darkness. It was Lucy. She was alive. She'd taken flight into the woods, they could only have been a short distance away from each other. They'd spotted her. She was running again, flushed out of her hiding place. And she was heading in the direction that they wanted, directly up to the river's edge. That's where they'd corner her.

$$8$$

One Week Before The Race

Lucy threw the last of Hamish's dirty clothes into the washing machine. It never seemed to end. How could one tiny person create so much crap? He wasn't even moving about properly yet, but already the house had been turned upside down and there didn't appear to be a corner untouched by some item of baby paraphernalia.

If she hadn't felt so disengaged by it all, she might have got the house tidied up in time. Sophie was due at eleven o'clock and then they were heading into town for a coffee. Clive had suggested it to Jack on the train up to Aberdeen, it had seemed like a good idea. It would get Lucy out of the village and give her some adult company for a change.

Lucy had been lost in thought for most of the morning. She'd been searching through properties on Rightmove, fantasising about a relocation to the town, or even better, the city. She'd attend toddler groups, maybe even get Hamish in daycare. If she could get him in a nursery, if she didn't have to spend every damn hour with him, perhaps she might be able to turn things around.

They could get a good-sized terrace in the city, somewhere with parking, and they'd perhaps make a bit of money on the house. Jack might be able to find work locally. Maybe things could work out.

Lucy struggled not to plunge herself into a downward spiral of depression. The house had had no interest for months. Only carpet treaders and locals keen for a snoop inside. Nothing serious.

Even if they did get a bite, how long would it take to move on? By the time any buyers had buggered around trying to price drop on the basis of the survey, it could be another three months. She wasn't sure if she could last that long. If it ever became too much, she had her plan.

Jack didn't seem to be listening to her. Not really listening. She had to get out. Out of that house. Out of that village. Out of that endless cycle of weekdays on her own. And away from Hamish. There, she'd admitted it to herself. It was Hamish she needed to be away from. He was suffocating her.

At least the running helped. Jack had been right about that. Out on the road, with or without Jack accompanying her at the weekends, she felt like her old self again. It's how they'd met. It seemed so long ago. The university running club. It was just the two of them back then, of course. Hamish – the twins – didn't come along for another ten years. She associated all the bad times with the pregnancy. That's when the business went bad. It didn't help that she had to finish work early because she was so sick in the mornings. And Helen, of course. She moved her mind off that topic, thinking about Helen took her to a darker place altogether.

Lucy had plotted it out soon after Jack started working in Aberdeen. Maxine was trustworthy. She'd call her in on a day when Jack was travelling back from Aberdeen. That way Maxine wouldn't get stuck with Hamish, Jack would be there to take him off her within a few hours. She'd order a taxi and tell Maxine that she was throwing out some old clothes that didn't fit her any more, not since she'd had the baby. That would explain the suitcase too.

'I'm getting rid of these at the charity shop!' she'd announce. She'd snapped straight back into shape anyway, but Maxine wouldn't ask any questions. She'd assume Lucy was seeing things when she looked in the mirror.

Instead of going into town, Lucy would head for the city. It would be a hefty taxi fare, but she'd been squirrelling away a small cash supply. She had enough to survive without using cards for a month if she was careful and got some shitty bedsit. One month. To sort her life out. And if it didn't work out? There was always the other option. The worst-case scenario. It wouldn't come to that, she was certain. If she could only catch a break and catch her breath.

Lucy heard a car door slam outside. She assumed it was Sophie. Sophie was ten years younger, still in her mid-twenties. Clive wasn't the marrying kind. He liked to keep a younger woman in tow, and he usually moved on when they raised the issue of babies. Maybe this was what the babysitting suggestion was all about – a chance for Sophie to see that having kids isn't all blissful bedtime stories and ball games in the park.

Lucy envied Sophie her youth and ignorance. If she could turn back the clock, she'd stay as they were. Just her and Jack, plenty of cash, lots of freedom, no kids. Sophie needed to be careful what she wished for.

There was a knock on the door, loud and confident.

'Hi Lucy. I'm Sophie. I'm so pleased to meet you. What a lovely place you have here, so nice to raise a family.'

Lucy bit her lip, she didn't want the first words out of her mouth to be a rant.

'Thanks for coming round, Sophie – and for you and Clive volunteering to babysit at the weekend. I ... we really appreciate it.'

'No problem at all. Where is the little guy?'

'He's over there, asleep in his pram. If we're lucky, he'll stay that way for most of the time we're out. He was awake half the night. That's why I look so rough.'

'Nonsense, you look fabulous. I hope I look as good after I have kids. You look in amazing shape.'

'Thanks. I think the running has helped. I seem to have lost most of my baby weight.'

'You're wonderful the way you run like that. Clive goes out when he's home, but it's not for me. I prefer the gym – chat with the girls and coffee afterwards. Much more my style. Speaking of which!'

'I tell you what, I'll ring Maxine and she can sit with Hamish while we pop into town for a coffee.'

Maxine was in. She could spare two hours. Sophie picked her up in the car and they left her at the house with a pile of textbooks to mind a sleeping Hamish.

As they drove around looking for a parking place, Lucy could tell Sophie was gearing up to ask her something.

'I'm pleased it's just you and me,' Sophie began. 'It's not that I didn't want to get to know Hamish, of course, but I wanted to have a chat to you about something.'

Lucy was shaken out of her daydream and now paying full attention to Sophie.

'I'm only asking you this because ... well, um, Jack and Clive know each other ... and they're a similar age ...'

'It's okay,' Lucy encouraged. 'I won't say anything to Jack.'

This seemed to give Sophie courage.

'When they ... when guys get to their forties, do they start to have problems ... down there?'

Lucy felt as if she'd stepped onto the set of a Carry On film. She wanted to burst out laughing, but she kept a straight face.

'It's not common at that age, I think, but that doesn't mean it won't happen. A fit chap like Clive, it shouldn't. Why, is there something wrong?'

'He just seems to have gone off s-e-x recently,' she continued. 'To be honest with you, I wonder if he's having an affair.'

Lucy couldn't get over how quaint Sophie was for such an attractive and confident young woman. She could tell she wanted to be listened to. It was hard to admit the truth and she was clearly bothered by it. She must have felt that Lucy could help.

'I don't know about Clive, but Jack is so tired after a week in Aberdeen that he's not really interested in anything at the weekends. He sleeps, we run, and he spends time with Hamish. Then it's back on the train on Sunday evening. Groundhog Day, I think they call it in the States.'

'But Clive ... he seems to making lots of secretive calls recently. He never tells me who it is. *Just work!* he says. But he's always so furtive. I think I might be losing him.'

Lucy knew that feeling alright, but she kept it to herself.

'It won't be you, it'll be a problem at work, I'm sure. Jack's always saying that Clive can't stop talking about you.'

Lucy enjoyed her short time in town with Sophie. They had a coffee, chatted through Sophie's concerns, and got to know each other better. She seemed young and a little naive to Lucy, but she instantly warmed to her, she could see that she had a good heart. Clive should hang onto this woman for dear life.

It wasn't long before they were back in the car again heading home to Hamish and Maxine.

'I hope you'll trust me with Hamish overnight. I know it's hard to leave them when they're so young,' said Sophie.

'Of course we'll trust you. Jack and I are really grateful that you and Clive are happy to come over. And being away from home might give you both a chance to talk. I'm certainly looking forward to having Jack to myself for the weekend.'

'I can't wait, honestly!' Sophie replied. 'I'd love a child of my own. Hopefully Clive will feel the same way sometime soon ...'

She trailed off as she realised that Lucy's attention was suddenly elsewhere. She had twisted round in her seat to look at a car that had driven past them as they'd turned into the lane that led to the house.

'What is it?' Sophie asked. 'Do you know them? Should I stop?'

Lucy was silent, craning her neck to be certain of what she'd seen. It was the same car that she'd been given a ride in the week before. It was the woman that she'd met in the cemetery. The road didn't go anywhere, it was a dead end. There was only one place she could have been, she must have been to Lucy's house. So what was she doing there?

9

———————

One Week Before The Race

Jack thought nothing more about his encounter with Anna in the washroom at work. He headed out into the car park. Clive was a fast walker and there was little chance they'd run into each other with such a good head start, so he was confident about going into town.

He called Lucy. The line was engaged. What were the chances of that? He'd hoped to catch her over lunch. He tried again. Still busy. Who would she be talking to at that time of day?

Jack slipped into a sandwich shop in the city centre and idly looked out of the window as his sandwich was being prepared.

'Do you want butter?' the girl asked.

'Yes please,' Jack replied, not really caring. 'Actually, better make that something low fat if you've got it. I need to take care of my six-pack!'

He smiled at her but she ignored him. Jack let her get on with it, and watched what was going on outside.

Shit! Clive! He was sitting on a bench across the road, deep in conversation on his mobile phone. He'd have to give him time to move on.

'I'll eat that here, please.' The girl nodded and moved the knife more aggressively over the roll.

Clive ended his call but didn't move. He seemed to be waiting for someone.

Jack's sandwich arrived. He added a bottle of still water, paid for it, and pulled up a chair at a table near the window from where he could survey Clive. As he tucked into his sandwich, he decided to try Lucy again. This time she picked up.

'Hey!' he said, his mouth full of ham. He'd half-expected it to be engaged still.

'Oh hi, I didn't think you'd call so early.'

She sounded brighter, but Jack thought he might be imagining it. She'd accused him of checking up on her the previous week. He was trying to strike a balance between showing his genuine concern and not making her feel as if she was being watched.

'Who were you chatting to just now?' Jack asked, immediately thinking better of it. Fortunately, she shrugged it off.

'Oh, nobody. You know, checking in with the estate agent. I was wondering if we'd had any more interest in the house.'

'Everything alright at home?' Jack queried, sounding as casual as he could. He always braced himself for the answer.

'Everything's fine, you know how it is,' Lucy replied.

Jack could almost see the clenched teeth. She was blocking him. Things must be bad again. He'd try and get home on Wednesday evening, if they'd let him. He would work late to make up the time.

'I could see you were out to lunch, Jack. That bloody wristband tracks you everywhere you go. You should turn it off sometimes.'

'I've got nothing to hide,' he replied. 'At least you can see I'm not getting up to any mischief.'

He'd forgotten about Clive. He glanced over to the bench. Clive was now in full conversation with an older man with squared glasses and a trimmed, grey beard. He wore an expensive jacket and looked sure of himself. Jack was no expert on body language, but their exchange seemed tense. Whatever was going on, Clive didn't have the upper hand.

'You there still?'

'Sorry, sorry, Luce. I was distracted.'

Then, from nowhere, hostility.

'Don't let me bother you too much. It wasn't me who rang, you know. You called me. You might at least have the decency to pay attention while we're talking.'

Where had that come from? He'd need to get back home, she was running on a short fuse. He had to stop working away, this was helping nobody.

Clive's hands were waving violently at the older man. Voices were raised. Jack tried to pay attention.

Lucy's outburst had woken Hamish who was now bellowing from the sitting room.

'Look, Jack. Ring back later, the baby needs me. Call me tonight when things have calmed down a bit, now is not a good time.'

She ended the call. She usually said goodbye. Not this time.

Jack felt bad, but couldn't keep his eyes off Clive and his companion. He texted Lucy quickly, a conciliatory message.

Love you x Sorry I was distracted. Will call this evening. Jack x

The man was trying to give something to Clive, but he didn't seem to want to take it. It was an electronic device, a large phone or a small tablet, something like that. Clive looked scared, not a look Jack was used to seeing from a man usually so boorish and cocky.

Whatever the older man had said to him, Clive finally acquiesced and placed the item in his coat pocket. There was no farewell, no shaking of hands. Clive took the device and strode off in the direction of the city centre.

Jack finished his sandwich but decided to sit sipping his water a little longer to see if he could get a better look at the man. He also wanted to give Clive a chance to get away. He'd have to think of a way of finding out what was going on without letting him know that he'd come into town after all.

The man sat on the bench. Every now and then he looked up and down the street. He must be waiting for someone.

There was a vibration on Jack's phone. It was a text from Lucy.

I'm sorry too. Hamish was just stirring. All quiet again now. Chat later xxx

Jack felt immediately better. At least it wouldn't be awkward when they spoke that evening.

He looked up. Damn, the man had moved on. Jack jumped up from his seat to see if he could see where he'd gone. He left the shop and looked up and down the street. It was busy, the offices had all spilt out for lunchtime, but he managed to pick him out in the crowd heading back into the centre. He had a companion with him, a woman. Jack couldn't be certain from that distance, but it looked very much like the woman he'd been speaking to in the washroom less than an hour previously.

He headed straight back to the office after his amateur surveillance session in the sandwich shop. He wondered who Clive had been talking to. Perhaps the man had a different role at Pharmexus, a colleague on a fact-finding visit who'd arranged to meet for lunch in town. But why had the conversation looked so tempestuous?

He had never particularly liked Clive, but it was a mutually convenient alliance which served them both. If he would only cut the bullshit and level with people, he'd be a lot more bearable. However, one thing he could say about Clive was that he never got riled. He always had a smart-arse comment or a one-liner to defuse any tension. He enjoyed airing his sexist and homophobic views as well as the occasional 'I'm not a racist, but...' comment.

This older man had been the only person that had ever managed to fluster Clive, certainly in the time Jack had known him. He worried the issue for the rest of the week and resolved to mention it when he got an opportunity.

10

Sunday 01:06

Shadows were moving through the darkness, hunters seeking their prey.

It was the woman who troubled Jack. He'd caught her name – Rosa. She seemed a lot less impulsive than the company that she was keeping. While the men moved ahead, itching for a fight, Rosa appeared to have sensed his presence. She was hovering near his hiding place, blocking him from moving ahead and getting closer to Lucy.

He wondered if he could overpower her. He'd not got a clear look at her yet, but in the darkness he'd mistaken her for a man. She was tall and muscular, her hair cut short and her face severe. He could tell that much, and he suspected he'd come off worse in any attempt to tackle her. Besides, he had no weapon, and they were heavily armed with knives and guns. He and Lucy didn't stand a chance.

Every so often he'd catch a glimpse of Lucy's fluorescent strips glowing in the torchlight. He cursed that she'd not thought to turn her clothing inside out, oblivious to the fact that she was giving herself away.

Jack moved quietly between the trees, all the time watching Rosa behind him. She was not involved in the hunt for Lucy, she'd let the others go ahead. Rosa had a different prey. He tried to pick out the voices in front of him, desperately trying to figure out what was going on.

Jack was troubled by the man they'd struck on the road. The horror of those events had subsided already, overtaken by the need to survive and stay alive. But the man had looked familiar. Could it really have been Matt Rackham? No, he must be mistaken. What would Matt have been doing in the middle of nowhere miles from Aberdeen?

Lucy had picked up the man's wallet in the road. That should settle the question of his identity.

Jack glanced over his shoulder. Rosa had gone. He'd been distracted, deep in his own thoughts. He had to focus.

He heard a voice call in the distance.

'You want her alive?'

He strained to hear the answer. He caught the tail end of it.

'... make it look like she drowned.'

Their relationship difficulties seemed trivial compared to this. He felt ashamed that he'd had thoughts of leaving her, wondering if he and Hamish could make it on their own.

They had killed the man in the car and now they were hunting down Lucy, they were covering their tracks. What could he do? They'd kill him too, he had no way to defend himself.

Scanning the woods for Rosa, Jack took cover behind a dense gorse bush. He had to somehow get ahead and reach Lucy before they did – and tell her to hide those damn fluorescents. They needed to get to wherever the phone signal kicked back in again. He daren't check his mobile, he was terrified it might light up and give away his whereabouts. He realised he'd left the volume turned up loud in case Sophie and Clive needed to get in touch about Hamish. It was the dead of night, they wouldn't call now. Surely not?

Where the hell was Rosa? He couldn't see her or hear her. Jack edged forward, desperate not to lose the main pack. He heard the sound of water – the river, at last. He'd make his way along the edge, at least they'd all be heading in the same direction.

He searched hard in the darkness for Rosa's outline, the fools ahead were giving away their whereabouts with their torches. He counted four of them, but it was difficult to tell.

Just Rosa on her own, who knew where?

The river was running fast, he cursed the recent heavy rain. The bank was steep, but not so steep that he couldn't climb down it. A twig snapped to his right. He almost missed the sound against the roar of the water. He crouched down, listening for any clue as to where Rosa was. Silence. He waited, it felt like minutes but it can have only been seconds. Then, the click of a weapon. Was that the sound guns make when they are cocked ready to fire? He wished he'd paid more attention to the countless American dramas he'd watched on TV.

There was shouting up ahead, they were closing in on Lucy.

'Over there, she's heading for the river.'

'Spread out along this stretch, make sure she doesn't cross.'

'Don't shoot. We need to make this look like a drowning. You got that Blake?'

If they weren't going to shoot, it would buy Jack time.

He'd have at least a small chance of getting to Lucy before they did. He could see from the torch lights that they were taking position dotted along the riverbank. If he could make it through a gap in the sentries and slip into the water he might have a chance of saving her.

He'd have to risk being seen by Rosa. Jack moved out wide, constantly looking around him, expecting at any moment to be spotted. He reckoned that, once in the water, Lucy would move with the current so she was more likely to be further down the river, not higher up. The group of men hadn't worked that out, so at least he had that advantage over them. For now.

Moving quietly through the woodland, he reached the water's edge. The trees were close together and the river was lined with bushes. He caught a flash of Lucy's jacket ahead as the torch beams swept across the water.

He stepped in up to his knees, it was icy cold and, even close to the bank, he could feel the force of the current. Cautiously, he moved from the side, unsure as to the depth, feeling for stones and firm ground on which to rest his feet. He would need to go in up to shoulder height. The less visible he was, the better.

Jack grabbed a handful of mud, twigs and foliage, debris from the river that had piled up against a fallen tree trunk. He rubbed the mud over his face and did his best to cover his head with the matted twigs and leaves. He wanted to laugh out loud at himself in the darkness and cold of the river, but he knew that to do so could result in the death of them both.

Slowly, he moved through the water, trying not to get pushed forward by the powerful current. If he could get to Lucy ... if they could safely make their way to the other side.

He saw her up ahead. He daren't call out. She was right

in at the side of the bank, ducking her head under the water whenever the torch beams scanned the river. He could hear the men calling to each other. They were getting annoyed and impatient, fearing they'd lost track of their target.

Jack was in whispering distance of Lucy when, from nowhere, Rosa leapt from the bank into the water. He was unsure for a moment if it was him she'd seen or Lucy. It was Lucy.

Rosa grabbed Lucy's head, as if to check it was her, and then pushed her face deep and hard back into the water. Lucy thrashed around, she couldn't breathe. Jack hurriedly looked towards the bank. The men were closing in on them. Rosa had made no sound, this was her kill, but the others had been drawn by the splashing of the water.

Jack had only a moment to act. Lucy wouldn't be able to hang on for long. Rosa hadn't seen him yet and the men were beginning to clamber down the bank. He had the element of surprise.

Rising out of the water, he lunged towards Rosa. He was cold and his clothes were heavy. He felt as if he was moving in slow motion. Rosa saw him coming and instinctively reached for her gun. It wasn't there, she must have left it at the side of the water to keep it dry. Her hand moved quickly to the other side of her belt where her hunting knife was sheathed, but the delay had given Jack the seconds that he needed. He crashed into her and she fell back into the river. Lucy's head ripped through the water, and she took a desperate breath, like a new-born baby entering the world.

'Come with me!' Jack shouted, taking her hand. She was fighting for air and she could barely see; mud from the river bed was caked across her face.

Rosa was regaining her footing. They had to wade

through the water as fast as they could. The men with the guns were almost upon them.

'Go Lucy, go! Don't stop, keep moving!'

Lucy was dazed, weak and confused, but she sensed Jack's urgency and began to fight her way across the river.

Rosa was on him already, her hands tightly squeezed around his neck. Her grip was strong, crushing his throat. He was fading already, but he forced a turn so that he could see that Lucy was getting away. Is this what it was like to die? If it was, it didn't seem too bad. He was becoming increasingly lightheaded, there was no pain now, just a sense of drifting away.

Then a shot – two shots. A thud in the water. A new voice coming from behind him. A body floating down the river.

11

———

One Week Before The Race

'This is important, Maxine. You'd better not be lying to me. Are you sure that no one called while we were out?'

Lucy was embarrassed that she'd lost her temper with Maxine and in front of Sophie too. The sight of the woman in the car had agitated her. What the hell did she want?

Maxine's face was red. She wasn't used to conflicts like this. Lucy immediately regretted laying into her so hard.

It was Jack who'd pushed for Maxine to babysit. He was so desperate to give Lucy a rest from Hamish, that he'd almost fallen over with joy when Maxine turned up unannounced on the doorstep asking for the work.

'But we don't know anything about her,' Lucy had protested, 'and she's probably never had any experience with babies.'

Maxine had spotted their ad in the community pamphlet that did the rounds of the three villages in their parish.

Childminder/babysitter sought for local couple. Must have references and previous experience. Up to four hours each week.

They'd had no response at first. The perils of rural living. Jack had begun to think they were going to draw a blank. Lucy felt the suggestion of getting someone else in to watch over Hamish from time to time was an insult to her mothering abilities, but Jack saw that she needed the break and he was determined to get this help.

Maxine turned up at the door on a Sunday morning. Hamish had obliged them by sleeping through the night and they'd just had Sunday morning sex, a ritual that they missed from their pre-child days. Jack answered the door in his boxers and a back-to-front T-shirt. Perhaps it wasn't the best way to begin a childcare relationship.

'Hello. Can I help you?'

The girl was thin and slight. He hated himself for noticing it, but she didn't look like she came from an affluent family. Her earrings were bright and made from plastic, her clothes plain and cheap. Jack wasn't a snob, but that's what struck him about Maxine.

Her face lit up when she spoke and he cursed himself even more for being so appalling in his assessment of her.

'Hi, I'm Maxine Sowerby. You wanted a babysitter?'

Her voice instantly revealed her bright and friendly personality.

Jack was caught off his guard. They'd put a phone number on the advert, why hadn't she called instead of turning up on the doorstep? Upstairs Hamish was beginning to wail.

'We were looking for a qualified childminder really.'

He heard Lucy cursing.

'Coming, coming, you little ...'

She didn't finish her sentence, but it didn't take a genius

to know where she'd been heading with that. They needed a babysitter.

'I do lots of babysitting in the village,' Maxine continued. 'I've got three references with me.'

Jack opened the envelope she handed him. It contained two handwritten notes and one typed on a PC. Each one explained how kind, caring and patient Maxine was with children. He scanned phrases like *the children love her* and *patient and reliable*.

'How old are you, Maxine?' he asked.

'Eighteen ... I'm going to university in January,' she replied. 'So you've only got me until then.'

'That's an odd time to go to university, isn't it?' Jack asked, intrigued.

'Yes, I'm a second-semester starter,' she started to explain, 'It's a long story, but I have a lot of studying to do before I go.'

Jack invited her into the house. Things seemed a bit tense between mother and child upstairs, so he ushered her through to the kitchen.

Jack had already decided that Maxine would be fine, but he asked a few interview-like questions to let her know that he was no pushover. As they spoke, each could tell that they'd made a good connection and the conversation turned as if having Maxine as their babysitter was a fait accompli.

Then Lucy entered with Hamish, who was squirming in her arms, as if she wanted him to settle in a place that he didn't belong. Maxine's eyes lit up when she saw him, and the baby reached out towards her. It must have stung Lucy to see that. She handed him over, a forced smile hiding the pain she felt.

The girl was a natural. As Jack watched her gently bouncing the baby on her knee and talking to him as if they'd been best friends forever, he wondered why Lucy had found that so difficult. Wasn't mother and child the most basic, primal relationship in the universe? So why did Lucy continue to struggle with it?

Lucy wasn't prepared to make the decision there and then. She told Maxine they'd discuss it and get back to her. Jack guessed that part of it was pride. In spite of how much she was struggling, Lucy still needed to show that she was Hamish's mother and she made the decisions about his welfare.

She went through the motions of asking after her in the village, but couldn't find a scrap of evidence on which to base a rejection. It was true that Maxine's father had never worked in his life, and the family lived in the only remaining social housing in the village that hadn't been sold off to its tenants, but no one had a bad word to say about her. She had always been the odd one out. She loved her father, he wasn't violent, but she aspired to something better in life. She was determined to get out of that village and create a better future for herself. The villagers gave her the encouragement and credit that she deserved for her youthful aspirations. When she minded their children, they'd sometimes slip her an extra fiver, telling her to add it to her university fund.

So, before long, Maxine was their babysitter. And even better, Lucy had accepted the help. It had eased the tension between her and Hamish and Jack felt better about leaving them in the week. Maxine was nice to have around too, she fitted in.

Which is why she felt so uncomfortable when Lucy lashed out at her. She'd never seen that side of her before. Lucy apologised, realising that she'd gone too far.

'How about I run Maxine back home and you put the

kettle on?' Sophie asked. 'If Maxine is taking the first shift with Hamish at the weekend, it makes sense if we chat beforehand. Is that okay, Lucy?'

Lucy was grateful for Sophie's help. She'd been a right bitch. It was the only word she could find to describe her behaviour. She slipped Maxine an extra tenner, apologising again as she squeezed the note into her hand. She couldn't really spare the money, but she needed to smooth things over.

Maxine said her goodbyes and she left the house with Sophie, as they'd agreed. Hamish was happily playing with a rattle on the rug.

Lucy thought about the older woman. What could she possibly want? She'd seemed nice enough. If she'd been driving down their lane, there was nowhere else to go, she knew that's where Lucy lived.

Lucy thought it through. Maxine was adamant that she hadn't called at the house. Was she checking out the property before putting in an offer? Had the woman intentionally run into Lucy in the cemetery with a view to getting more information about the house sale? Perhaps she was chasing a deal, seeing if she could place a stupid offer.

Lucy decided to check the phone to see if the estate agent had called with an update. Maxine was good like that, she always passed on messages but Lucy had barely given the poor girl a chance to draw breath before she'd started shouting at her.

The phone had a call log. There had been two calls while she'd been out. One was from Jack. He'd rung the house first and then caught her on her mobile while she'd been enjoying a coffee with Sophie. Nothing urgent, just quick call to say hello. And check up on her.

The second call was not a number that she recognised. It

had an Aberdeen code, but it wasn't Jack's firm. She googled it, watching as Sophie drew up outside the house and walked up to the door. The Aberdeen phone number didn't register as being a business or domestic line, it must be ex-directory.

Sophie stepped through the front door, which they'd left ajar.

'Okay if I come in?'

Lucy beckoned her in, slamming down the lid of her laptop.

'She's a lovely girl that Maxine,' Sophie said. 'Very ambitious, she clearly wants to get out of this village. I guess there's nothing here if you're a young person.'

The falling out with Maxine was forgotten. Sophie was cooing over Hamish, Lucy was chatting away with her new friend, and the mystery phone call was forgotten.

It wasn't until the day after the half-marathon that Lucy would get to stare into the cold eyes of the man who'd asked for that call to be made.

12

———

Two Days Before The Race

It was Thursday evening and Jack was relieved to be heading south again, albeit with Clive as a travelling companion. It was two days before the run. Sophie had met Hamish and Maxine, and he and Lucy were all set for an adult weekend away together. They needed this.

Jack was plying Clive with drink. The advantage of travelling First Class was the free booze. Clive always took a taxi from the station, so Jack had no qualms encouraging his travelling companion to drink up.

'How are you looking forward to your child-minding duties on Saturday? Are you all prepared?'

'Sophie can't wait,' Clive replied, taking a swig of beer. 'She loves your little one. Got on really well with Lucy too. Reckon we've created a couple of new mates there.'

'So you're taking over from Maxine on Saturday morning, is that right? I know Lucy and Sophie have it all arranged between them, but I wasn't really listening properly.'

'Yes, they do witter on at times, don't they?'

And there it was, the Clive who couldn't stop winding Jack up.

'We'll be there on Saturday to take over from Maxine, and you're back by 8am at the very latest on the Sunday?'

'That's right. We'd have liked to stay over, but I'll drive back overnight on Saturday. We appreciate you and Sophie stepping in.'

'Sorry we can't stay for Sunday. A night away with the wife, well I would if I was you!'

Why was it that Jack always ended up wanting to punch Clive. He changed the subject.

'Who did I see you talking to in town the other day – an older guy with glasses and a beard?'

Jack had chanced it, but Clive hadn't consumed enough booze.

'Was that the day you stood me up for buying your lunch – the day you weren't supposed to be in town?'

Jack covered quickly.

'Lucy called and asked me to pop into the bank. She'd had a problem with one of her cards.'

It was a half-truth. She *was* having problems with her cash card, but he'd contacted the bank about it by phone the day before. Clive bought it.

'Only a guy who wanted some figures from me. He was visiting the firm.'

'Looked a bit heated when I saw you.'

Clive looked uncomfortable, then recovered quickly.

'Yeah, yeah, you could say that. I was pissed off at him. He was chasing me for some information that I'd said I'd have ready for later that day. He caught me at the wrong time. I was on my lunch break for fuck's sake. It could have waited!'

This explanation didn't ring true, but Jack wasn't sure if he should push it any further. He risked it.

'He looked a bit threatening. You seemed to be having a proper argument.'

'Look mate, are you my mother or something? I feel like this is the Spanish Inquisition all of a sudden. We had words, we straightened it out later, alright? It was nothing, just some pain in the arse leaning on me. I'm off for a piss. When I get back, let's change the subject, eh?'

Clive got up and walked down the train carriage towards the toilet. Jack felt like a dirtbag, he'd change the subject when Clive got back. Besides, if he upset him it might scupper his weekend away with Lucy. Running was always a safe topic.

Clive got back and sat in his seat. He picked up the conversation as if nothing had happened.

'Every time I unzip, even I can't believe what an impressive specimen I am. And to think Soph gets a full weekend of it, lucky her!'

It wasn't quite the topic of conversation that Jack had hoped for, but at least it wasn't going to mess up their weekend away. He let Clive drivel on about the size of his manhood for a few minutes, and then artfully directed the conversation towards running.

Even though he spent much of his time wanting to punch Clive's lights out, Jack would never have wished on him the events that were about to unfold over that weekend.

PART II

PREY

13

———————

Sunday 01:23

Jack looked around in the darkness, desperate to see if the body was Lucy. There was shouting, panic, confusion. Damn the roar of the water, it was difficult to make anything out.

'Come with me if yer want ta get oot o' here!'

There was a man in the water beside him. Dressed in camouflage gear, he was older and carrying quite a bit of weight. He spoke with a strong Glaswegian accent.

'Stop fucking about, yer numpty. If yer don't move yer arse fast, you'll be the next 'un floating downstream!'

Jack started moving across the river to the furthest bank and the man moved with him.

'Yer lassie is ahead of us, she's fine. But these buggers are tooled up. Ma wee shotgun won't be much use now.'

Jack strained his eyes. He made out Lucy's silhouette in the distance.

All hell was breaking out at the side of the river. He

could just make out what was being said over the sound of
the water.

'Shit, the bastard shot Tanner.'

'Stefan, Arne, follow them across.'

'She's okay, just dazed. Pull her over to the side—'

'Do not, repeat, do not terminate the target.'

Was it him they were after, or was it Lucy? 'Terminate
the target' sounded like a Mission Impossible movie.

Without warning, something heavy struck the back of
his head. It was a branch which was being swept along by
the current. He lost his footing, fighting to stay conscious
and to keep his head above water.

'Woah!' came the voice to his side. 'Yer almost made me
drop ma friggin' gun!'

The man had caught Jack's arm. He'd seen the log at the
last moment and hadn't had time to warn him.

'You alright?' he asked, not releasing Jack's arm until he
was certain that he was steady, 'cos if yer not, we're in shit
street.'

He looked behind him. Stefan and Arne were closing in
on them. These guys were not experiencing the same problems crossing the river. They were tall and muscular, and
seemed accustomed to the hostile environment.

'Yeah, yes, I'm fine. I can stand. Can you see Lucy?'

'Keep walking, yer nelly. She's doing fine. You might
want ta take a wee leaf oot of her book. If those two
Germans catch up with us we're goners.'

This was no time for talking. They were now closer to
the opposite bank of the river, they'd almost made it.
Torches were sweeping across the water. Jack kept catching
glimpses of Lucy's fluorescents. He made out her figure
ahead, clambering up the bank. He was aware of the men

behind them, they seemed to cut through the water effortlessly.

Jack hit a hollow in the river bed and stumbled, his head dipping under the water. He surfaced with a mouthful of weeds and paused to splutter and catch his breath.

'Do yer not understand this, soft lad?' the man at his side shouted. 'If those buggers catch up wi'us, it's curtains. What is it yer nay understand about that?'

Jack pushed ahead, forcing his body through the swirls of the water and driving towards the river's edge. At last they were there. Lucy had spotted them and was waiting with an outstretched hand.

'Jack! Jack! Grab my hand, quick, get up here!'

Jack reached out and grasped her cold, wet hand. She was freezing. He'd been so preoccupied with getting across to the other side, that he hadn't even thought about how bitterly icy it was in there.

Lucy helped him climb up the bank. It was good to feel his wife's skin again as he held her hand. As he stood up, she threw her arms around him, holding him tight.'

'Thank God you made it. I thought I'd lost you—'

'A wee hand here, if yer don't mind!'

Jack and Lucy broke off and worked together to haul the Scotsman out of the water. Jack's limbs were stiffening as the immersion in the river water began to take its toll. His clothes were sodden and heavy, his movements slow.

Still the torches swept the water. Arne and Stefan were making good progress behind them, they probably only had a five-minute start.

'What the fuck is going on – and who are you, appearing from nowhere?' Jack shouted at the man.

'A "thanks for saving ma life" would do! Listen to me, and

make sure yer listen properly. You two are going ta get through the trees and then yer'll come to a field. Head diagonally across the field to the wee barn. The door is open, there's a quad bike in there. The key is under the old paint pot on the shelf. You'll see it. It's easy enough to drive. Make yer way along the track at the side of the barn, as far as the gate right at the end. That's where the track meets the road. I'll meet yer there. Wait behind the hedge, make sure it's me.'

'But what are you going to do? And who are you?' Lucy blurted out.

'I'm Calum. I was hoping for a quiet wee night o' poaching but I walked in on a rammy. I'm going to draw these two buggers away from you, along the riverbank. Ma van is parked at the bridge, I'll lose them there. The others will be following doon the road. And wee lassie, will please take yer hi-viz thingummy off and turn that bloody jacket of yours inside oot, they can see yer a mile away! I'd have got to yer half an hour ago if yer didn't keep popping up like some daft Jessie.'

It was Lucy's turn to look sheepish now. She removed the bib, dropping it on the ground, then turned her jacket inside out, as Jack had done earlier.

'Come ta think o'it, I'll use this t'draw them away,' said Calum as he picked up the clothing. 'Run, you two. Get t'that quad bike. I'll meet yer at the road and we'll get us some help.'

Jack and Lucy looked at each other, then headed through the trees in the direction that Calum had indicated. Jack glanced back to see him standing on the riverbank throwing stones at Arne and Stefan as they waded through the water.

'Come on, Luce. If Calum poaches this land, he'll know

what he's talking about. Are you okay? You must be freezing.'

'I'll survive. Let's go, we need to run.'

There were no torch beams now and they could only hear faint shouts behind them. The trees were not thick on this side of the riverbank and they soon emerged into fields. What had Calum said? Head diagonally. Jack had lost all sense of where they were in relation to the road. They'd have to trust him. Jack wondered if Calum would prove any match for the two men pursuing them. He was a big guy, but not in a marines-kind-of-way like the men who were hunting them. There was no way he'd be able to outrun them once they reached the safety of the riverbank. Maybe that was why he was throwing objects at their pursuers, buying time to salvage precious minutes.

Lucy and Jack jogged in silence. The night was still, there was the occasional bleat from a sheep in the distance. Moonlight was breaking through the thinning fog.

'Do you have your phone, Luce?' said Jack, feeling in his pockets for his own.

'I dropped it in the woods when that first shot was fired. I panicked and ran. I'd been checking for a signal. We can't be a million miles away from the next village, surely?'

'I've got mine,' Jack said. They'd slowed down to a walk, but they had to keep going, they couldn't afford to stop. He tried to coax the screen into life but it was dead.

'Shit, I think the water's got to it. See if you can do it, my hands are so cold I can't feel the buttons.'

They walked on, listening constantly for hostile or threatening sounds. Nothing.

'It's knackered!' Lucy cursed in the darkness, throwing it onto the ground. 'I thought these bloody things were supposed to be waterproof.'

'They're not indestructible,' Jack replied, picking it up. 'I'll hang onto it. It might fire back into life when it dries out.'

'I can see the barn!'

Lucy was running fast now. Jack put the phone in his pocket and caught up with her. It was exactly as Calum had described, although he'd neglected to mention a second side-door, which they were unable to budge. The main doors of the barn weren't padlocked, and they were soon inside.

'No electricity,' Jack said, feeling around in the darkness for a switch. 'Can you see the quad bike?'

'Over here!'

'It's so dark in here. I'm going to open the doors to get as much light in as we can.'

Jack pulled both doors open. It wasn't a lot of use but it helped them to figure out the basic geography of the area. The quad bike was under a tarpaulin, it would have been helpful if Calum had mentioned that.

Lucy made her way over to the shelf and felt around for the key. It didn't take her long to find it.

'Have you any idea how to drive these things?' she asked.

'Not a clue,' said Jack, but I'm guessing that I have no time to take lessons. Unless you want to give it a try?'

'I drove one once, remember? On that girlie weekend away before we got married. Shall I drive? It's ages ago, but I think I remember how it works.'

'Be my guest,' said Jack, allowing her to position herself on the seat. He tucked himself behind her, moving in close. They needed the warmth. They were both shivering uncontrollably.

Arne and Stefan were only minutes behind them. If

Calum failed in his diversion attempts, they'd be upon them soon.

Lucy inserted the key and gave it a turn. The quad bike was dead.

'Try it again!' said Jack, desperate for the bike to start.

'I did, it's dead.'

'Shit! Any idea what it might be?'

'How should I know?' Lucy snapped.

'Let me take a look,' said Jack, climbing off.

He cautiously felt around the engine. Jack's knowledge of cars ended at filling up the water bottle for the wipers, but as a teenager he'd cut neighbours' lawns using petrol-driven mowers, so he'd had some experience at nursing reluctant machines into life. A rubber cap was moving freely against his hand.

'It's the spark plugs, the farmer must have loosened the cap as a security measure. I'll see if I can work it back on. There it is. Give it a try.'

Lucy turned the key and the engine roared into life. So did the lights.

'Luce, turn them off for God's sake!'

'Piss off, Jack. They'd been left on by the last driver. If you think you can do better, you drive the bloody thing!'

'Sorry, I'm sorry, Luce. I'm just a bit ... tense. We both are. I'm sorry.'

'Come on, Jack. We need to get out of here. Jump on the back and let's see if we can make this thing work. We'll drive without lights. Agreed?'

Jack removed the discarded tarpaulin from the front of the vehicle and clambered back onto the bike, putting his hands around Lucy's waist.

Cautiously, Lucy began to move the vehicle forward through the barn doors. The idling engine was quiet, but as she grew accustomed to the feel of the throttle, it would occasionally roar loudly.

Jack kept his mouth shut. He was grateful that his wife even had a clue how to drive it. They scanned the area, praying that Arne and Stefan would not be there. There were no shots, no shouting and no movement. It seemed safe.

Lucy began the drive along the track. She was getting the feel for it, although the brakes were sensitive and every so often there would be a jolt. The track was full of potholes. They were picking up speed and Jack quickly learned to brace himself for the bumps.

There were no lights and no torches behind them. They hadn't heard shots for some time. The track went on for a mile or so, that made sense to Jack. They had to clear the river and pass the bridge. He hoped that Calum had his geography right. Lucy kept the quad bike in second gear, it was a comfortable level, fast enough but not too loud and not too much revving.

Soon they reached the five-bar gate which marked the beginning of the road. Lucy brought the bike to a halt and left it idling.

'This must be it,' she said. 'We'll need to open the gate to get to Calum, or will that give the game away, do you think?'

I don't see that we have a choice,' Jack replied. 'And if anything kicks off, we can take the quad bike out onto the road and make for the village.'

They worked together to pull back the gate, lifting it over some big stones which were in the way.

'Shall I leave the engine running?' Lucy asked.

'Yes, we might need it. Let's tuck it into the hedge. If anybody other than Calum comes along this road, we need to stay out of sight.'

Jack and Lucy leant against the side of the quad bike, looking up and down the road, waiting to see headlights come round the bend.'

'I'm so cold,' Lucy said. 'I can't stop shaking. My hands are almost rigid.'

'Put them near the engine. It'll be warm enough by now to act as a heater, but don't touch it. You did so well there, Luce. Thank you for driving.'

Lucy moved closer to Jack and held her hands over the engine.

'Have you still got that wallet?' Jack asked, as they waited.

Lucy said nothing, but fumbled in her pocket, reluctantly removing her hands away from the warmth of the engine.

'Yes, at least I managed not to lose that. Why?'

'I need to see who that guy was that we knocked over. It can only have been a couple of hours, it feels like forever already. Can I take a look?'

'Can you see in this light?'

There was an ignition lamp on the quad bike, it gave off enough light for Jack to be able to see. He had a good rummage through the wallet.

'I'm taking his cash. If we ever get to civilisation, we're going to need that. Ours was burned in the fire.'

He dug deeper. There was a picture of the man's family, a smiling wife and two young children. It had stayed reasonably dry inside the inner pocket.

'There's a driving licence. This is what I wanted to get a look at ... I thought so! He works for Pharmexus in Aberdeen. His name is Matt Rackham.'

'Did you know him? What was he doing out here?'

'I've only seen him about the building. He's involved in

the big project that I've been working on. Different departments, you know how it is, but I know him. That can't be coincidence, can it?'

'Are you saying this is connected with your work? What the fuck are you doing up there? Boring tech stuff you told me.'

'It is, just tech work. I'm no pharmaceuticals expert, you know that. What I'm doing is all very secretive, but that's nothing out of the ordinary. I'm always signing NDAs. I never even bother to read them

'Are you sure about that guy? Matt ... what did you say his name was?'

'Rackham. And yes, I am sure. I didn't recognise him at first, he was in such a mess when he was lying on the road. It was when I was running to get help that I began to suspect that I knew who he was.'

'Where did the men come from? They must have arrived soon after I left. I heard the gunshot.'

'There's an older man with them, he didn't follow us into the woods. Or at least I didn't see him. Franz, they called him. He's the leader – the others are the muscle. And that Rosa woman. Shit, I wouldn't want to run into her on a dark night.'

'You just did!'

Lucy laughed nervously.

'What's this all about, Jack? What do they want? They were shooting at me. At first they were trying to take me hostage, but when I ran off I'm sure they were trying to kill me.'

'I think it's me they want, Luce,' Jack replied. 'They don't seem to want me dead, but I have no idea what it's all about.'

'I didn't tell you before; I thought you'd tell me I was seeing things. There was a woman in the village a couple of weeks ago. You know how sometimes you notice people? They're not up to anything, but they stand out. That's what this woman was like. She didn't belong. And she lied to me too.'

'What are you talking about? Hey, here's Calum!'

The conversation was curtailed. A van was making its way along the road, driving slowly, searching for something – or somebody.

'What's his van like? Did he say?' Jack asked.

Lucy began to move towards the gate.

'Luce, wait! Let's make sure it's him first. Wait!'

She ignored his pleas. She was cold and desperate to get inside the van so she could warm up. She hadn't taken much notice of the vehicles that had pulled up in the road earlier. Calum had said he was driving a van – this had to be him.

She walked onto the verge and waved. She was dazzled by the headlights as the van pulled up alongside her. From his position crouching behind the hedge, Jack heard the sound of the handbrake being applied and the door opening. Carefully, hesitantly, he peered around the side of the gate. As his eyes began to adjust to the glare of the headlights, he realised that they'd just given themselves away.

From behind the passenger door stepped a tall, muscular figure. It was Rosa. And within seconds she had her hands around Lucy's neck.

14

———

Lucy was gasping for breath. Rosa stared at Jack, daring him to try and stop her. The driver got out of his side of the van. It wasn't the older man Lucy had mentioned, he was one of the guys who'd been hunting them down in the woods. The one with the small dick. Blake.

Suddenly there was the screech of brakes and the crunch of metal as a second vehicle crashed into the van from behind. Blake leapt into the ditch at the side of the road. Rosa instantly loosened her grip on Lucy's throat.

'Lucy, run!' Jack shouted. The quad bike was still idling behind the hedge. He jumped into the driver's seat and felt for the pedals. Lucy got on behind him, still fighting to catch her breath. She knew that she had to flee if she wanted to stay alive.

'Where's the fucking clutch?' Jack screamed. Rosa was coming through the gate towards them.

'There. There! Push it with your foot. Go. Go!'

The quad bike roared into life. Jack drove straight at Rosa. She saw the look on his face, he would drive over her if he had to. She jumped out of the way as the quad bike bumped over the verge and hit the surface of the road. Instantly, the drive became easier and they picked up speed. Rosa rushed out behind them, raising her gun and firing two shots. Jack drove faster.

'How fast can these things go?' he shouted, his eyes fixed on the road ahead, scouring it for obstacles.

'Where are the lights?'

'There, to your right!' Lucy reached past Jack to point at the switch, holding his waist tight with her other hand.

'Fuck! They're coming!' she screamed.

Behind them she could hear the revving of an engine as Blake pulled the van off the bumper of whoever had just rammed it from behind.

'Step on it, Jack! It should do sixty easily. Thrash it.'

'If we come off this thing, we'll turn our heads to mush. We aren't even wearing helmets.'

'Jesus, Jack, you're driving like your mum!'

Jack took her cue. He moved through the gears and the wind whistled in his ears as the bike gathered speed. They were flying along the country lane faster than he would have even dared in a car.

'Jack, they're behind us. Go faster!'

The full-beam lights shining behind them illuminated the road ahead.

'She's got the gun pointing at us. Swerve, Jack – don't drive in a straight line.'

'But that'll run us off the road!'

A bullet hit the right-hand wheel guard.

'Shit!' Jack cried. Twisting the throttle as far as it would go, he began to veer from side to side. They were travelling at over 60mph.

'They're gaining on us. You've got to go faster. You're in fourth gear, get it into fifth, we can squeeze more out of this thing!'

In her panic, Lucy was trying to reach over and take the controls.

'Jack, look! Over there – we're running parallel to the motorway. If we get onto it we can shake them off. They've got phones on the hard shoulder.'

Lucy stood up and reached past Jack to take the wheel. She wrenched it to the left, aiming for a field gate a short distance ahead. The quad bike lurched and bumped along the verge, coming to a sudden stop.

'Lucy, what the fuck are you doing?'

She jumped off the back of the bike and started to pull open the gate.

Their manoeuvre had taken Blake by surprise. He over-shot the gate and braked so hard that he skidded onto the verge. He tried to reverse, his front wheels spinning in the mud.

Lucy opened the gate and waved Jack through.

'Come on! They won't be stuck there long.'

Jack turned the bike towards the gate and Lucy jumped back on.

'You want to drive?' he asked, beginning to rev.

'No time. Come on, let's go!'

The van was now out of the mud. Blake swung it towards the gate. Jack was driving across the field at full throttle.

'How are we going to get out of here, Luce? We're trapped!'

'No, look, over there. They're repairing the fence. It's that orange stuff they use on roadworks. You can drive straight through it. Come on, Jack, they're catching us up.'

The glare of the van's lights was behind them. They had no choice but to make for the gap in the fence. It was about two metres wide, the orange mesh held up by three metal posts. Jack aimed between two of them and shut his eyes as they drove through the fencing at high speed. It collapsed under the weight of the quad bike and they hurtled down the embankment onto the motorway.

Jack moved up through the gears, the van behind them following every step of their desperate journey.

'We're driving against the traffic, Luce. We'll be pulverised if we meet a lorry.'

'Keep going. It's the dead of the night and we're in the middle of nowhere. As soon as we see a service station or a turn-off, we'll leave the motorway.'

It made sense, but Jack was terrified by their speed. They had to be going 70mph, it felt like 100mph with the wind in his face. He kept on the hard shoulder, hoping that it would provide at least some protection if they came across a vehicle that was heading north.

'They're on the motorway now. They're closing in, Jack. Oh for fuck's sake!'

'What? What?'

Jack dared not turn around, he was going too fast, a swerve in either direction and he'd flip the bike.

'There's a second van following us. It has to be one of theirs.'

Jack turned the throttle even harder, but they were going as fast as they could. In his peripheral vision he saw a van moving out to their side, while the lights of the second were only metres behind. They were going to try to force them off the road.

The motorway was heading downhill. Jack saw a blue sign on the other side of the road – it must be a turn-off or perhaps a service station. Tightly contained on the hard shoulder, one van on his tail, the other at his side, Jack concentrated on the road. He had to keep the quad bike steady. Lucy had stopped shouting, she was frantically looking behind and to the side.

Suddenly a car came in the opposite direction along the slip road. Seeing three vehicles heading straight for him, the driver veered towards the main carriageway, forcing the first van to swerve in front of the quad bike. Jack braked hard only to be bumped by the other van behind. He swung the bike into the side of the hard shoulder.

The van behind careered across the motorway exit into the curving metal barrier alongside the slip road. There was a thud as the quad bike clipped the edge of the hard shoulder, spun in the air, and sent them hurtling into the darkness. Then came the sound of a crash and a dying engine. Everything fell silent.

15

———————

Sunday 02:03

On the slip road from the services was evidence of a multi-car pile-up, but there was a calm and stillness, as if those involved hadn't worked out what had happened yet. There was little traffic on this rural stretch of motorway through Scotland on a Saturday night.

The first sound was a groan, then the metallic noise of a seatbelt being unclipped and the click of a door. It was like an awakening, as one person regained their wits, another would be roused to consciousness by their movement.

On the grass bank beside the slip road, Lucy opened her eyes and scanned the area ahead. It was the indicator light that drew her gaze first of all; it was dangling by a wire but still flashing. It was the car that had been exiting the services, signalling to enter an empty motorway. The driver, a woman as far as she could tell, was slumped over the steering wheel. There was no airbag, or it hadn't inflated on impact. The front of her car was completely wrecked by the crash.

She looked for Jack. He was lying on the ground several metres away from her. He was dazed, but moving. They were alive at least. She heard the noise of a van door opening – there was movement among their pursuers. Lucy looked for the quad bike. It was upside down, right across the slip road, on the far verge. Not a chance. They had guns, she'd never make it.

All of her instincts made her want to check on the welfare of the woman in the car. What must her thoughts have been as she emerged from her short break at the services to see two vans and a quad bike heading at speed towards her on the wrong side of the road? It must have been terrifying. But there was no time for reflection. She had to make a move.

The door of the second van was pushed open. Lucy and Jack were hidden in the shadows, but the men would soon be after them, and that woman – Rosa – the worst of them all. She would want payback, Jack had humiliated her in front of the men. She would not easily forget how his inept attack in the river had allowed Lucy to get away from her.

Jack groaned. Lucy crept over to him.

'Quiet, Jack. They haven't seen us yet. We need to move away from here. Are you okay?'

'I banged my head when I came off the bike. It feels as if I've been hit with a sledgehammer. Is it bleeding?'

Lucy inspected his head. It was hard to see in the semi-darkness.

'You've got quite a deep gash, but it's not bleeding too much – your hair has got matted in with the wound. Can you move? We need to get away.'

Jack stood up slowly, testing his arms and legs for any further injuries.'

'I'm good. I can run. How about you? Is your ankle up to it?'

'It's not so bad. It's sore, but I ran through the pain in the woods and I'll be able to do it again.'

Constantly glancing back, Lucy and Jack worked their way to the top of the bank away from the lights of the service station. It was dark there, so long as nothing came that cast a shadow on the road below, they'd be fine. They could hear the voices of the men in the distance. They were regrouping. An engine started, then a second. Both vehicles must still be driveable. Jack stopped to take a closer look.

They jumped as the crack of a gunshot cut through the night.

'Shit, they just shot that woman in the car!' Lucy gasped. 'What do these people want? Look, they're pushing her car off the road behind the bushes.'

'Lucy, come on. We have to get out of here. We need to make our way round to the back of the services and call the police. And don't forget, there's always the chance that Calum has already alerted them.'

They jogged along the top of the grassy bank. On the slip road below, the quad bike was being lifted over the barrier and onto the verge.

Where was Calum? He hadn't made it to the roadside as planned. Had he been killed by Arne and Stefan when they got out of the river? Was it him who'd given them their chance to escape when Lucy had stepped out into the road too soon and been seen by Blake and Rosa?

'For fuck's sake!' Jack exploded, as the services came into view. It was just a petrol station and shop, with a café in a separate building. He'd hoped for something bigger, somewhere they could hide while they waited for help. There was one lorry and a single car in the car park, and no sign of life inside.

Engines were revving behind them. The men were on the move. They had to get to the services and raise the alarm. They sprinted down the bank and into the car park.

Suddenly Lucy's leg buckled.

'Damn! My bloody ankle, it just went again!'

'Come on, put your arm around my shoulder. We're nearly there.'

The two damaged vans screeched into the car park behind them, their headlights on full beam.

'Hell! Oh no. Come on, Lucy. Head for the door to the shop.'

Seven figures emerged from the two Mercedes crew vans. They were putting black masks over their heads with neatly cut eye and mouth holes. This was no amateur operation. These people had come prepared. They were not going to get identified from CCTV footage.

Jack and Lucy made it to the shop. They burst through the door, scanning the area. There was nobody at the tills. There were four rows of shelves packed with crisps, sweets, de-icer, screen wash – the usual items that line the shelves of petrol stations.

'Hello! Hello! Anybody here?' Jack shouted.

A toilet flushed in a backroom behind them.

'Jack, they're here!' Lucy whispered. 'We have to take cover.'

They could hear the sound of the hand dryer.

'We need to warn them, Jack. You know what they did to the woman in that car.'

'I'll try and get to the back room, you hide over there, behind that shelving. Let's hope the assistant has a phone. If we get separated, where shall we meet? Back at the slip road where we left the quad bike? They won't think about going back there. Meet me there if we get split up. I love you, Luce. I know things have been difficult ... you know I love you.'

'I love you too, Jack.'

Lucy looked at him, then moved away to crouch down behind some two-way shelving that was used partly as a window display. To her side was a fire exit. She could use it to make her escape if she had to.

Two figures burst into the shop, their faces obscured, handguns at the ready. They hadn't seen Jack and Lucy go in, the men had split up into groups, they were searching the entire service station for their targets. Jack was on all fours, making his way towards the open door of the back room. He would do his best to avoid detection, but there weren't many places to hide.

The hand dryer stopped. They heard the latch of the toilet door slide across and the assistant began to make his way back to the shop.

16

He was just a young guy, probably no more than twenty years old. He was humming to himself. The night shift was always quiet – the occasional customer topping up with fuel, maybe buying a bar of chocolate and a can of coke.

As he walked back into the shop, he stopped humming. He had his head down, concentrating on his mobile phone. When he looked up, there were two hooded figures standing by the till and, down to his left, crouched on the floor, was Jack, his finger to his lips.

His eyes gave the game away, of course. Jack knew he was wasting his time, the poor chap was scared out of his wits.

'You can take the money!' he said, his phone falling to the ground. 'Take whatever you want. Please don't hurt me. Help yourself to whatever's in the till.'

He was pleading for his life. He'd seen the weapons that they were carrying.

'Come out of there!' shouted one of the men. Jack recognised his voice, it was the one called Stefan.

'You stay still,' said the other, training his gun on the assistant.

Jack reached out to grab the discarded mobile phone. He put it in his pocket alongside his own damaged unit and began to crawl back to the end of the row, away from Stefan.

The other man, Arne, as far as Jack could remember, was standing by the door, blocking the exit.

Jack looked over to where Lucy was hidden. She was well-concealed, but it was only a small shop, they wouldn't last long in there. He looked around for something that he could use to defend himself. He grabbed a can of de-icer. It might buy a few seconds if he threw it. He flipped off the lid – perhaps the spray would be useful.

'Mr Dawson, you need to come out please!'

They still weren't certain that he was even in there, they were chancing their luck, hoping to flush him out.

The English was good, but he spoke with a German accent.

Stefan reached the third row of shelving as Jack tucked himself into the second. He couldn't be seen by Arne. But they could only play cat and mouse for so long.

'We only need to speak with you, Mr Dawson. Can I call you Jack? This needn't be any worse than it is already.'

Were they calling his bluff? Did they know he was in there? Jack didn't know. He remained silent.

'Look, Jack, we both know that this can only last so long now. So why not put us all out of our misery and give yourself up? You can't escape from us and we only want to talk.'

Jack thought about Matt Rackham's body burning, about the shooting of the woman driving along the slip road. He thought about how they'd chased him and Lucy with guns.

'Here's a little encouragement,' came Stefan's voice. Jack's ears rang with the crack of a gunshot. He heard screaming. It was the shop assistant.

'What's your name, boy?' Stefan shouted. 'Stop your bloody snivelling or next time it won't be your foot but your head I put a bullet through. Verstehen Sie mich? You understand me?'

Jack couldn't breathe. He wanted to gasp for air and vomit at the same time. The assistant was trying hard to stifle his cries of pain, doing his best not to antagonise Stefan any further.

'It's Michael – Mikey. Please don't hurt me. I'll give you anything you want.'

'Stand up, you motherfucker!' Stefan commanded, and Mikey did his best to comply. Stefan held his gun to Mikey's head.

There was a movement close to the fire exit. It was Lucy, looking pale and shocked by what she'd witnessed. She looked across at Jack and pointed towards the fire exit. He nodded, holding up his hand for her to wait a moment.

'What is it you want from me?' he said.

They knew he was in there now, but what could he do? He had to consider Mikey too, he'd seen what these people were capable of.

Arne began to move towards the source of the voice, but Stefan told him to wait.

'We need to speak to you, Jack. You're a difficult man to get an appointment with. You have caused us a lot of trouble tonight.'

'Let Mikey walk out of here, then we can talk. He's no part of this.'

There was a moment of silence. Jack dared not look above the shelving to see what was happening.

'Please, let me go. I won't tell anybody. Please, my foot hurts, let me go.'

Jack heard the sickening sound of Stefan's gun handle strike the side of Mikey's head. He screamed out.

'Behave like a man!' Stefan sneered. 'Walk over to the door.'

Jack heard Mikey limping towards the entrance.

This time Arne spoke.

'Okay, Jack, when you step forward, Mikey walks out of the door.'

Stefan was moving up the aisle towards Jack's hiding place. He'd have to make his play soon. If he was manoeuvred towards the first row of shelving, he'd be too far from Lucy and the exit.

'Stay where you are, Stefan. I'm going to stand up slowly. When I stand up, you let Mikey walk, then we talk, okay?'

'Alright, Jack, have it your way. I am stopping now and I am placing my gun on the shelf. Arne, you know what to do.'

Jack looked at Lucy. Her eyes were urging him to be careful. Jack held out his hand warning her not to do anything yet.

'Okay, Stefan. I'm standing up. Now let Mikey go.'

When death comes, it can come in the blink of an eye. With Jack now out in the open, Arne and Stefan struck quickly, a well-oiled machine. For Jack the horror seemed to play out in slow motion.

Mikey's hand was resting on the door handle – he thought his ordeal was over. Arne raised his gun to Mikey's head, pulled the trigger and blew the top of his head off.

Stefan was primed and ready. He hurled himself towards Jack. Lucy called out to warn him, giving him just enough time to raise the can of de-icer that he was holding and spray it in Stefan's face.

Lucy pushed down the bar on the fire exit. It opened out onto the back of the building.

'Jack, over here. Hurry!'

His face splashed with blood and brain, Arne levelled up his gun and pointed it directly at Lucy. She turned to face her killer.

Stefan was thrashing around on the floor, trying to locate Jack with one hand, rubbing his eyes with the other.

'Lucy, run!' Jack screamed at her. Arne was going to kill his wife. They had no intention of sparing her, it was him they were after.

There was a flash from Arne's gun as he fired at Lucy. At the very same moment his chest exploded into a mess of red, the glass in the door shattering.

Lucy screamed as the bullet whisked past her, splintering the glass of the fire exit. Jack turned to kick Stefan in the face. He was only wearing trainers, there was limited damage that he could do to a man of Stefan's size, but it was enough to keep him down for a few moments longer. He grabbed Stefan's gun and looked over towards the broken glass from the shop door. Arne's body was now lying on the floor on top of Mikey. Outside stood a big, burly figure. He strode into the shop.

'Fuck these arseholes, can't a man get a wee drop of petrol around here?'

It was Calum. And he'd decided to show his face just in the nick of time.

17

———

Sunday 02:33

'Calum, this way!' Lucy shouted.

She was watching Stefan. He was now unarmed, but he was a powerful man, and a determined one too. They would be no match for him.

Jack rushed up to Lucy, inspecting her as if he couldn't quite believe that she was unscathed. Calum stepped over the two bodies and struck Stefan on the head with the stock of his shotgun. He slumped to the ground.

'There are lots of them, I counted another five, they're like ants,' Calum said, barely drawing breath, 'too many for us to take on. They're in the café and the forecourt, making sure yer not hiding oot there. There's some poor lorry driver taken a bullet. I thought it was you.'

They went out of the fire exit into the night, moving towards the darkness at the back of the building. There were industrial bins there, contained within a brick enclosure, far enough away from the buildings to provide a temporary hiding place. They ducked in behind the bins. From there they could see that the vans had been left in the car park, their doors wide open.

'What happened to you, Calum? You didn't meet up with us when we'd got the quad bike,' said Jack.

'I managed to shake off the two laddies who followed us across the river. And it was me who bought yer tha time to get oot o'there when yer walked oot right in front o'them by the gate, yer wee dobber. And I can tell yer that Rosa is pissed with us. I've spent time in Glasgow and I never heard language like that. What's all this aboot? They keep saying yer name.'

There was a shuffling noise behind them. Calum's hand moved to the knife attached to his belt. It was a middle-aged woman wearing an apron. She'd taken refuge at the rear of the building too. There weren't many other options for staying hidden.

'Are you okay? What's your name? Can you tell us what happened in there?' asked Lucy.

'I'm Erica,' the woman said. 'I was having a cigarette and checking my phone out the back when I heard a loud bang. They killed him, they killed Travellin' Bill. He's a lorry driver, he owns that lorry in the car park. He comes in here for an early breakfast before heading over to Hull on his weekly run. He's done it for years ... and now look at him!'

She began to cry. Lucy put her arm around the woman's shoulders trying to quieten her.

'Did you hear what they wanted?' Jack asked.

'I didn't hang around,' Erica sobbed. 'They didn't see me. They didn't know I was there. I was waiting for them to leave. Then I heard more shots.'

'That was me,' said Calum, 'but I'm shooting the bad guys, dinna worry. And ta think I was hoping to come home with a couple o' wee rabbits or some pheasants, a deer if I got lucky. I've been poaching those woods for years but I've ne-er seen the like of this before. A couple of those wee buggers were oot in the woods a week or two previous. I wondered what they were up to – assumed it was drugs.'

'This has to be connected with Aberdeen, Jack. What are you doing up there? You've pissed someone off,' said Lucy.

Jack had remembered Mikey's mobile phone and was nursing it back into life.

'For fuck's sake!'

'What now?'

'It's bloody fingerprint recognition. The phone is on, but I can't use it.'

'You'll be able to make an emergency call, won't you?'

Jack checked the screen again.

'You're right, Lucy, nice one. There's still a crap signal though. One bar.'

'You won't get a decent signal here,' said Erica, who was now calmer.

'Here, take mine, but it'll be no better than Mikey's. There's a phone in the kitchen and one by the tills. Land-lines. They're a better bet up here.'

Jack took the phone and saw that she was right, it was no use right now. He handed it to Lucy for safekeeping, looking to Erica to get her approval. She nodded, relieved that someone else was around to sort things out. Jack tucked Mikey's phone away to the side of the wall, the police would want to see that later, no doubt.

'Where are the nearest police here?'

Calum and Erica snorted in unison.

'Twenty miles away at least,' said Calum. 'We haven't had proper policing around these parts fer years. Why do yer think I'm oot poaching? It's rich pickings fer all.'

Calum held out his shotgun. It reminded him to reload. It was no threat to automatic weapons, his gun was for hunting animals, not men. He expertly placed two cartridges in the chambers and snapped shut the barrel.

'Just in case,' he said. 'Yer saw what two barrels did to oor friend back there.'

'I have Stefan's gun,' said Jack, 'but I'm not sure I could even use it anyway.'

'You might have to,' said Lucy. 'Look, they're regrouping. There's that Rosa bitch. How many of them? I count six.'

The four of them strained to get a look into the car park. It was difficult to tell at that distance.

'What about that lorry driver?' said Lucy.

'What aboot him?' Calum asked, looking into the distance, worried at what was being planned over in the car park.

'Could we escape in his lorry? Or what about your van, Calum?'

'I left it way back up th'road. No way I was announcing ma arrival.'

'A lorry will be harder to drive than that bloody quad bike,' Jack interrupted. 'Erica, do you have a car?'

'No, I don't. My husband drops me off and picks me up. Mikey's car is out there in the car park, though.'

'We can't get to Mikey's body to grab his keys. There's too much glass in the shop window, they'll see us from a mile off. How about we try to get Travellin' Bill's lorry keys?'

A short distance away from them on the tarmac their hunters were splitting off into search groups.

'Come on, Calum. You and I can creep around the back and into the café.'

'What about us?' said Lucy, indignant that she was being excluded.

'You need to rest your ankle,' Jack replied. 'You and Erica can take Calum's shotgun and we'll have the handgun – it'll make them duck for cover if nothing else.'

Lucy nodded and made sure Erica's phone was still safe. Calum quickly showed them how to cock and uncock the shotgun.

'Yer've got two chambers, ladies, two shots maximum. These wee things make a mess close up. Good luck!'

Jack hugged Lucy. She hesitated for a moment before responding. She'd felt isolated for so long that she'd almost lost the instinct to be close to his body.

The two men began to move through the darkness towards the open kitchen door. They could see it as soon as they emerged from the bins, the back of the café was unlit, it was easy enough to get there. They heard voices, the area beyond the buildings was now being searched.

As Calum and Jack neared the kitchen door, the area flooded with a bright light. Damn, a movement sensor. They'd have to take their chance and go in anyway. The damage was done now, they'd have to hope that nobody saw it.

The kitchen was brightly lit. There was an industrial deep fat fryer gently bubbling away alongside the wall. A large metal catering bowl was full of batter in the food preparation area. Erica had been in the middle of preparing meals for the day ahead. All the clutter of a working catering environment was ranged along the worktops.

Carefully, quietly, the men made their way through the kitchen to the door to the café. All was quiet. They appeared to be alone. Jack gasped when he saw Bill's body. He was slumped over his fry-up, a newspaper on the table bright red with his blood.

'Stay here, Calum. Take the gun, keep an eye on both doors.'

He kept low, crawling along the floor for the second time that evening. He didn't want to risk being seen through the windows, it was like a goldfish bowl in there with all the lights on.

He made his way over to Bill's body, repulsed by the sight of his corpse. He wanted to scream seeing the old man like that. He felt in his pockets: matches, cigarettes, tissues. Finally, the keys. He'd expected them to be bigger. He had no knowledge of lorries, he hoped that Calum would know what to do. He seemed like the kind of man who might.

'I've got them,' he whispered. 'Everything still clear?'

Calum raised his thumb to indicate that all was well. Crouching low, Jack made his way across the café. Back in the safety of the kitchen, he held the keys up for Calum to see.

'Okay, we need to create a distraction. I take it you know how to drive that thing?'

Calum nodded.

'I used ter drive them for a living years ago. It's been some time, mind you. But aye, I'm sure I can get us oot of here. If I screw it up, ma van is parked up along the hard shoulder. We can always switch vehicles if we make it that far—'

'Shh!' said Jack. He had heard a click. Was it the safety catch of a gun being released?

The sensor light outside the kitchen door had just been triggered once again. They were not alone. There was someone outside and they were about to walk straight in on them.

18

Sunday 02:45

They had no alternative but to hide. There was no way they could fight this man. If they fired the gun, the others would descend on the café in no time.

Calum climbed into a metal locker which contained some chef's whites and what must have been Erica's coat. He pulled the door as close as he could, leaving a slight gap so that he could keep an eye on what was going on. He felt naked without his shotgun, but did have his hunting knife in its sheath. It would make a quieter kill if it came to that.

Jack couldn't conceal himself so easily. Looking around frantically for a space to hide, he ended up having to squeeze behind a hot cupboard, which was the only solid object in the room that wasn't pushed against a wall.

A man walked warily into the kitchen, expecting trouble. Jack hardly dared to breathe. He edged towards the side of the metal unit, getting a fix on the man's whereabouts. It was Blake. He was built like a brick shit house, there was no other way to describe him. The people hunting them, whoever they were, appeared to be grouped. There'd been Arne and Stefan and Blake and Tanner. Two Germans and two guys from the UK. He'd heard someone use the name Johnson too, he was one of them. Then there was Rosa and the older man who seemed to be in charge. She worked alone.

Tanner had gone floating down the river, and Arne's innards were now decorating the walls of the shop. That left Stefan, who'd been rendered unconscious with the butt of Calum's rifle. There had been more people than that in the car park. How many were there? Jack did a count in his head: Rosa, Blake and Stefan made three, but there had been six of them in the shadows of the car park.

Blake was moving cautiously, although he'd been careless enough to leave off his ski mask. Maybe they'd scoped the place and made sure there was no CCTV. He made a quick assessment of the area, checking the café too to be sure that he was on his own. He was distracted by the food. It had to have been almost 3am, Jack had lost track of the time. Blake picked at some sandwich fillings that had been left covered in cellophane on one of the counters.

Jack silently moved back behind the hot cupboard, watching in horror as Blake approached Calum's hiding place. He was going to open the door. Could Calum see what was happening?

Suddenly he heard a crackling noise, a walkie talkie. It was a voice Jack hadn't heard before, older and self-assured, with a German accent. This man was in charge. His English was good, but he was German, Jack was certain of that. He listened to their exchange.

—How is the kitchen area, Blake? Are you clear?

—I'm running a final sweep. There is no one here, only

the dead guy in the café. You want me to clean things up before we go?

—Nein. No. Just be certain Dawson is not there. I want him alive and unharmed, you understand?

—That might be difficult, this bastard is putting up a bit of a fight. How about his wife, you still want her dead?

—Keep her alive for now, we may need her to apply more pressure. Once we have him, she's useless to us. The others – kill them. I don't want any tracks left. There's no CCTV here, only over the petrol pumps. Johnson has sorted that out.

—How long have we got, boss? Six o'clock we have to go, yes?

—No delays, we have to fly out at 06:30. It's going to be tight. Don't fuck this up, Blake.

What did they want? Jack scoured his mind for clues. He was tech, not research or product development. He knew pharmaceuticals was big money, but he was a tiny part of the project.

Blake had finished the call and was placing the walkie-talkie in its holder. He hadn't forgotten that locker. If he opened the door, Jack would have to act. He still had the handgun. He scanned the area, the sound of the gun firing would only bring the others running, there was no way he could shoot.

There was a large sharp kitchen knife over by the sandwich meats where Blake had been picking at the food. It was to the side of the fryer. If Blake discovered Calum, he could run to it and use it in any fight. There was no way they were taking Blake down without a weapon. He was twice the size of them, his arms bulging with muscle, his neck as thick as a tree trunk.

Jack silently cursed as Blake readied his gun and swung

the locker door open with his free hand. Calum didn't give him a moment to think. He had his hunting knife at the ready, he'd gently eased it from its sheath as Blake had been on the walkie-talkie. He'd gone out for a quiet night's poaching, but instead of being the hunter, he had become the hunted. And now he was fighting for his life. He thrust his knife right through Blake's gun hand.

'Fuck!'

Blake screamed and the gun fell to the floor.

Jack got hold of the kitchen knife from the worktop. They had to take this predator down stealthily, like wolves hunting at night.

Blake was quick to recover, he knew the score here. It was kill or be killed. He thrust his left hand towards Calum's neck, squeezing his throat with such a force that he dropped the knife.

Jack moved towards Blake. Calum's face was bright red, he had no air. Blake had done this before, his victim was paralysed and fighting for breath. He slammed the door of the locker shut, never loosening his grip on Calum, pushing his victim against the metal door, sliding him upwards so that his feet were no longer on the ground.

Jack had to move fast. Blake had seen him coming, his bleeding hand ready to fend him off. In a moment of helplessness, Jack did something that would have looked ridiculous in a movie. Instead of lunging at Blake with the knife, he swept out his left hand and hurled the bowl of batter mixture directly at his target.

It went everywhere. Blake's head and eyes were covered with the stuff. He was temporarily blinded. He released his grip on Calum, who dropped to the floor gasping for breath. Blake thrashed around, trying to clear his eyes. He was edging backwards, on the defensive now. Jack ran towards him clutching the knife, only to slide on the batter mixture, which was dripping on the floor. He tumbled down hard, landing next to Calum.

As Blake cleared one eye, he saw his opportunity. Jack was trying to get up, his hands slipping on the floor. Calum was struggling to breathe, he was in no state yet to put up a defence. Blake kicked Jack in the stomach, sending him flying across the room, his head striking the side of the fryer as he landed. He felt the spit of hot fat. The pain was excruciating; he was completely winded, it was as if Blake was wearing concrete blocks on his feet.

Blake strode towards Jack, clearing his other eye. The batter mixture was dripping from his head. Jack knew that they wanted to take him alive. That was his one small advantage.

Blake was rushing towards Jack now. It was like being stampeded by a bull. Blake grasped his top and lifted him off the floor.

'Enough!' he screamed right into Jack's face.

'You stop now or that bloody wife of yours gets fucked up the arse before she dies. Okay? Now just settle—'

The slam of the frying pan just missed Jack's face, but caught Blake directly on the side of his head. Still he didn't relax his grip on Jack. Calum leapt onto Blake's back, pounding his arm with the pan. Jack kneed him in the groin, narrowly missing the hot fat of the fryer as he reached out to steady himself.

'Calum!' he called, pointing towards the fryer. Calum got the message straightaway. He dropped the pan, and before Blake had time to turn around, they seized his arms and tipped him forward thrusting his head deep into the bubbling fat of the fryer.

'Hold the bugger down!' Calum screamed, as hot steam began to pour from the bubbling mess of Blake's head.

Blake's hands and legs were still thrashing wildly. Burning fat splashed over Calum and Jack, but they ignored the pain, holding him firmly until he stopped moving. They had to make sure this giant of a man was dead.

'Okay?' Jack asked, looking intensely into Calum's eyes. There was a bloody, red mark around Calum's neck where Blake had been clasping him. It was a wonder he hadn't crushed his windpipe.

'Okay,' Calum nodded. They released their grip on Blake. His head slid out of the fat and his limp body fell to the ground. He was dead, his face a burned mess.

'I fancied a fry-up for ma breakfast, but I think I'll settle for cornflakes noo!' said Calum.

Jack started to laugh uncontrollably.

19

Sunday 02:36

As she watched Jack and Calum making their way over to the café, Lucy felt for Erica's phone in her pocket. Would the signal be good enough now to let her contact the police? She had to try.

She keyed in 999.

The phone was ringing. She could hardly believe her luck.

'Hello, emergency. Which service do you require?'

'Police!' Lucy whispered, keeping her voice low so as not to draw any unwelcome attention.

'I'm sorry, I can't hear you. Please would you repeat your answer – fire, police or ambulance?'

Lucy turned in the direction she'd been facing when the call had been picked up, the signal seemed to be stronger that way.

'I need to speak to the police. It's urgent.'

'Putting you through now.'

Just for a second, Lucy thought the nightmare might be ending. A new operator picked up.

'Hello, where are you calling from?'

'Where are we?' Lucy whispered to Erica. 'Where do I send them?'

'Shhh!' Erica made an urgent gesture to Lucy to shut up. She pointed, then held up two fingers. 'In front of the bins,' she mouthed.

Lucy cursed to herself, two people were coming up to search the refuse area.

'Hello, where are you calling from please?'

Lucy couldn't risk a reply. All she could do was turn the speaker volume right down so that the operator would be able to listen without the sound of her voice putting them at risk. Would they be able to figure out where they were from the signal?

Lucy and Erica slipped behind the heavy bins, concealing themselves just in time. Two figures appeared and Lucy heard the crackle of a wireless device. They were using walkie-talkies. One of them was the woman – Rosa. She was with a man whose voice she hadn't heard before. He was talking about the football match he'd been watching earlier that day. Rosa was radiating disinterest.

'Shut the fuck up, Olaf,' she hissed. 'And keep your eyes peeled. That's what you're getting paid for, okay? Let's deliver the package and get out of this godforsaken place.'

Lucy was terrified. They were hiding on the other side of the bins, concealed only by the brick enclosure. Would they hear the operator's voice as she talked on the phone? Lucy's finger hovered over the red button, but she couldn't bring herself to terminate the call. While it was still active she had a lifeline. She placed the phone back in her pocket, it would stifle the speaker, at least. If anything happened, it might make it easier for the police to track their location.

Shit! They'd left the shotgun at the side of bins. Erica hadn't taken it. She was empty-handed. Lucy pointed and Erica scrunched up her face. They were about to give the game away.

There was a scuffling noise to Lucy's right. She couldn't make out what it was.

'Hey, Olaf, over here. It's the big guy's shotgun. They were here. Be careful, search these bins.'

How long until they found them? Seconds? A minute maybe? Lucy looked around for options. She could push the bin and make a run for it. She could leap over the brick enclosure, it would buy her a few seconds of cover. There were a couple of wine bottles left by the bin at her side. If she broke one, at least she'd have a weapon. But what about Erica? There were two of them to get out of there. The decision was made for her.

The noise that she'd heard was a rat. Startled by the sound of the bin lids being lifted, it had also realised that the game was up. It made for the safety of the wall, to its surprise found Lucy crouched there and leapt at her throat, thinking that she was an attacker. Lucy shrieked. It was a reflex. She couldn't help herself.

Rosa grasped the handles of the heavy industrial bin and rammed it hard slamming Lucy's body against the brick wall. As she drew back the bin to thrust it at the fugitive a second time, Lucy tore the rat away from her top and threw it at Rosa. Its long fleshy tail brushed her face as the rodent flew through the air directly at Rosa's head.

There was a flash of light and a thundering bang. The rat disappeared in an explosion of flesh as its tail slapped Rosa's face before dropping to the ground.

'You fucking idiot!' she screamed at Olaf, who had picked up Calum's shotgun and hit it with two cartridges before it even struck its target.

'I've always wanted to try one of these things,' he replied, grinning stupidly.

This distraction was all that Lucy and Erica needed. As she stood up, Lucy felt a twang in her ankle. It had to hold, she was going to need all of her speed and stamina to get away.

'Over the wall, Erica!' she shouted, but Erica made the wrong call. She opted to go around the side of the bins.

She ran directly into Olaf, who dropped the shotgun and took a firm hold her neck before the weapon had even hit the ground. With the precision of a killer, he placed one hand on her chin, the other on the back of her head, and gave a sharp but firm twist. She crumpled and fell to the ground.

'Better, idiot!' Rosa smiled at him. 'Now let's get this bitch.'

Olaf took out his handgun.

'Prick!' said Rosa, as she brushed his gun to the side. 'The boss needs her alive – for now, until we get Dawson. Then we can play with her.'

Olaf put his gun in its holster and began to run after Lucy, with Rosa close behind. As they pursued her down the incline, the operator, thinking the drama was over, began to speak, her voice coming from the phone in Lucy's pocket.

'Hello caller, are you able to give me your location? Hello caller?'

With the voices now gone, she closed the call, assuming it to be a prank.

Lucy ran. She had to get to the lorry. That's where they'd said they'd meet. It was too late for Erica, she'd had moments to react, but a single wrong turn and she'd lost her life. Lucy was heading back towards the petrol station. She knew that Jack and Calum had gone to the café, but there was no movement over there. She had seen their pursuers spread out, searching the site in an attempt to flush them out.

She was tired and every limb craved rest, but she had to make this last effort a run for her life. There were trees to her left. They were conifers, planted in neat rows, not like the mixed woodland they had run through earlier. She would use them as cover, run wide along the edge of the car park, then make a dash for the lorry when Jack emerged from the café with the key.

She veered off to the left, the decision made. She knew that Rosa and Olaf were not far behind her. The running was much easier here than when they'd been pushing their way through the undergrowth that had stifled the woods earlier on. The pine needles formed a soft bed and the consistency of the planting meant that she could cross rows of trees and quickly get out of the line of sight of her pursuers.

Low, spiky offshoots protruding from the trees whipped across her face. Her cheeks were streaked with blood. She didn't care, she had to make that rendezvous at the lorry. The hill was sloping gently downward and Lucy knew that if she carried on she'd reach the verge alongside the car park.

She was breathing evenly and clearly now, her route was direct enough to get into a rhythm. For a moment she felt as if she could have been running on the open road along from their house, their place of sanctuary. How she craved that refuge right now, with Jack and Hamish. How could she have ever wished it away?

Lucy came to a stop, she'd reached her destination, a

little further along than she had intended. Although she could hear Rosa and Olaf cracking twigs behind her, she had a decent head start. The car park was clear. The lorry was there, pointing forward, ready to drive straight out of that hellhole. All she needed now was that signal from Jack.

20

———

Sunday 02:59

Jack picked up Blake's gun and his walkie-talkie. Calum was clasping the other gun firmly in his hand.

'There was a shot. Did yer hear it when we were fighting?' Calum asked.

'No – yes – probably. I heard something. I was too busy with our fried friend over there.'

'Yes, it was ma shotgun. Not a handgun. I ken its sound. It must have been the women firing the shot. We'd better get to the lorry.'

The security light outside the back door was off, so at least they knew there was nobody lurking immediately outside.

'Careful now,' said Jack, as he put his head around the back door of the kitchen to check that the coast was clear. He stopped and looked back towards Calum.

'How are we going to let Lucy know that we're ready? We need a signal.'

'Wait a moment,' Calum said, moving back over towards the locker where he'd been forced to hide.

Within moments, the fire alarm was sounding.

'Let's get oot o'here,' Calum said. 'I saw it when that wee bastard was trying to strangle me. If we're really lucky, it'll be hard-wired into the nearest fire station. Dinnae get too excited though, there's not a lot that's hard-wired oot here.'

Calum and Jack headed out of the back door and towards the trees that surrounded the edges of the car park. Sometimes being in the middle of nowhere brings advantages. This would provide great cover for them. Besides, the alarm would draw their enemies like wasps to jam. It was a good distraction.

'Okay, this is as close as we're going to get without being seen. Get the lorry started, Calum. I'll hide behind Mikey's car and cover Lucy and the woman from the café, Erica.'

Jack tossed him the lorry keys and began to make his way across the car park.

It wasn't a huge area, but with just the lorry, Mikey's car, and the two vehicles left by their pursuers in it, it seemed like a wide-open expanse to Jack. There was very little cover if shooting started.

He scanned the perimeter for Lucy.

There was a commotion over at the café. He could see through the large windows that the fire alarm had had the desired effect.

Don't get cocky, he said to himself. There are more of them out here and Lucy isn't safe yet.

Then he saw her, but she'd already seen him making his way across the open space to Mikey's car. Moments afterwards she spotted Calum heading for the lorry.

Jack waved at Lucy. She'd need to start running now, the armed gang that had gathered in the café wouldn't stay there for long, they could spill out into the parking area at any moment.

Lucy got the message and began to run.

'Hurry, Lucy!'

As Jack watched her, willing her to get to the lorry as fast as she could, he saw the men making their way to the front door of the café. He turned to look across the car park. Someone was running. At first he thought it was Erica, then realised it couldn't be. Rosa. It was Rosa. Where was Erica? Was she dead too?

Jack left his hiding place by Mikey's car and sprinted towards the lorry. Rosa would have to run like the wind to catch his wife. He could open the passenger door and get Lucy safely inside before she caught up.

Calum fired the engine into life, spurring him on to run faster. Jack put his left foot onto the metal step, opened the door and climbed up into the cab. It was bigger than he'd imagined. He'd never sat in a lorry before.

Calum revved the engine, itching to drive off. Across the car park, the men emerging from the café had seen what was going on and were readying their guns. Jack looked behind him. Lucy was still running, she was nearly there.

'Jump up, take my hand, Luce!'

She'd done well, but Rosa was fit and fast. She was gaining on Lucy, they'd only just make it.

'Start to drive. Slowly,' Jack turned back to Calum, 'really slow, don't leave Lucy behind. When I've got her, floor this thing, alright?'

Lucy was almost at the lorry. There was a shot. The moment she turned she knew she should have kept running, but it was instinct. Her ankle gave way and she faltered. Another shot. She hadn't been hit. Who were they firing at?

She knew Rosa would be gaining on her. Forget the ankle, forget the pain, if she didn't move now they'd have her. She lunged forward, ignoring the stab of cramp that shot through her lower leg. She was there, the lorry had begun to move, Jack had his hand out. She grabbed it, Jack pulled her up towards the cab and for a moment she thought she'd made it.

But as Calum began to accelerate, Rosa jumped up at Lucy, hanging onto her like a limpet, fighting to get Jack to release her. Calum revved the engine, sensing that it was now or never. Jack would have to shake off Rosa, they had to keep moving.

As the lorry picked up speed, more shots rang out into the stillness of that horrible night. Lucy did all she could to punch Rosa away with her spare hand, hanging onto Jack for dear life.

'Get her away, get her off me!' she screamed, fighting for her life.

With his other hand Jack reached out for his gun, which he'd placed on the shelf in front of the passenger seat. Every time Rosa pulled on Lucy to drag her off the step at the side of the lorry, the movement tugged Jack a little further away from the weapon.

Two shots. They were close. Jack didn't know where they'd come from. They distracted Rosa too. She stopped clawing at Lucy long enough for Jack to grasp the gun and point it towards her. He tightened his finger on the trigger, hoping that the weapon would be ready to fire, while the lorry careered across the car park.

He squeezed the trigger as Rosa gave one almighty pull at Lucy. The two women tumbled to the ground, rolling along until they came to a stop. The lorry revved, then went hurtling towards the trees at great speed. Jack pulled himself back into the cab, dropping the weapon onto the asphalt below. Calum was slumped across the wheel, the back of his head blown away by a bullet.

The window of the lorry cab was shattered. As Calum's foot slid off the accelerator, the lorry slowed to a halt, just short of the trees on the far side of the car park. In the large wing mirror Jack could see men running towards him, guns drawn. It was over. He didn't care any more. He'd done a terrible thing. He could see her lying still in the car park, a short distance from Rosa, who was now standing up.

He'd meant that bullet for Rosa. He'd fired as the two woman fell hard to the floor, for all he knew he'd shot his wife. He'd failed. It looked like it was all over.

PART III

DECEPTION

21

———

Sunday 03:07

It was an unusual thing to observe, given the nature of what had just happened, but all Jack could think of for a moment was how quiet things could be in the middle of such mayhem. Not for the first time that night, he was in the centre of a nightmare that he couldn't have even contemplated twenty-four hours beforehand. And there was absolute silence, only for a couple of seconds, but it felt like an eternity.

Calum's bloodied body was slumped at his side, a spattering of bright red covering the curtain behind them. It had been instantaneous. One minute Calum was talking to him, the next he was dead. If death came to him that night, Jack hoped it would be as fast as it had been for the man who'd come to his rescue.

Metre by metre, Jack began to scan the area around him. To his side, a body. Ahead of him the lorry lights shone out into the car park. To his right, the vehicles belonging to his pursuers. In the heart of them, his wife, lying still on the ground, as motionless as Calum.

Jack wanted to cry. He'd had enough. He was wrung out. And now the horror of what had happened was beginning to break its way through the flow of adrenalin. He'd let them take him now. Whatever it was they wanted, was it worth all these deaths? And who was he to be worthy of living when so many innocent lives had been lost?

They'd take what they wanted and kill him. He saw that now. Nobody was living through this. Whatever they were after, it was of a high enough value for them to kill. Jack was ready for it. He hadn't the will to fight any more, not with Lucy gone.

The man approaching him was carrying a gun – of course he was – and he looked confident and cocksure. They knew they'd got him. They were clearly used to killing, it didn't seem to concern them.

He could see that bitch Rosa. She was responsible for Lucy's death. That bullet had been meant for her. And now must have shot his own wife.

Olaf was almost upon Jack now. He would have to make up his mind. Would he go quietly, or would he fight it out until the end? He wanted to rest, he needed it to be over now.

He'd forgotten Hamish. What about Hamish? He'd be orphaned before he even reached his first birthday. He'd never know his parents.

Olaf was at the front of the lorry signalling him to open up. Jack pressed the button to activate the central locking; he needed to be alone with his thoughts a little longer.

'Open the fucking door or I'll put a bullet through your head!'

Jack was confident enough to know that they wanted

him alive, for the time being at least. He was Patient Zero in all of this, they wanted him for something important. It had to be to do with pharmaceuticals.

Ahead of him, he saw a movement. He leant over Calum's body and changed the headlights to full beam. Olaf held up his hand to shield his eyes, cursing Jack once again. The gun was raised directly at Jack's side of the windscreen.

There was a radio crackle in the lorry cab. He watched as Olaf responded to the call. Jack could hear the conversation – of course, he had Blake's walkie-talkie! He'd dropped it on the cab floor. He rummaged around trying to figure out where it was. It was with Blake's gun, Calum had stored them safely before he'd started up the lorry.

—Steady, Olaf. I want him alive. We've got him now. He'll come out in good time.

The voice was older, more considered and confident. Whoever this was, he was in charge. Then, a few feet away from whoever it was speaking, a voice. A familiar one.

—Jack? Calum?

It was Lucy. He could see her right ahead. She was dazed, but moving. She must have only been knocked out by the fall from the lorry. Rosa had rushed straight over to her, gun at the ready, always alert.

Jack found the walkie-talkie and pressed the orange button at its side.

—Lucy! I'm in the lorry. I'm coming to get you!

Olaf had climbed up to the footplate now and was beating the glass on the side window, determined to get in.

Jack pulled Calum's body over towards the middle of the cab, dropping him into the gap between the seats. He was heavy, a dead weight, and it took all of Jack's strength to move him.

There was a crash as Olaf smashed the glass on the

passenger's side window with the handle of his gun and thrust his arm inside the cab. The angle was awkward, but he was fumbling for the button which would manually unlock the door.

'Fuck it, fuck you!'

Jack calmly took Olaf's arm as it thrashed about at his side, and pushed it deep and hard into the splintered glass. Olaf screamed, but continued to fight. Jack rotated the now lacerated arm, twisted it, then pushed down as hard as he could onto Olaf's elbow. He felt the bones crunch. Was it broken or dislocated? He didn't care. This is what psychologists mean when they talk about fight or flight. They'd forced him into a fight now, and he was going to take it to its conclusion.

Jack climbed over Calum's body and sat in the driving seat. The engine was still running, the handbrake off and the gears in neutral. Olaf was standing in front of the lorry clutching his injured arm, a stream of expletives coming from his mouth, many of them in German.

Lucy was now on her feet, Rosa was holding her arm. He placed his foot on the accelerator. He'd expected the pedals to be bigger, but sitting in the driver's seat, it felt much like a car. He revved the engine. It was automatic so he didn't have to work out how to operate the gears. He moved the dial into Drive and the lorry slowly began to move forward. Crazed with pain, Olaf was too busy hurling abuse at him to realise what was happening. Jack seemed to recall that automatics had something called kick down, he and Lucy had had great fun with it in their single days when they were on holiday in Greece. They'd used it to overtake other cars, it could give a real speed boost when you needed it.

Well, Jack needed it now. Olaf had finally realised what was going on. Although the windscreen had been shattered by the shot which killed Calum, Jack was still able to look him directly in the eyes. Olaf turned to run towards the safety of his colleagues.

'You won't be able to hide over there, you little bastard!'

Jack floored the accelerator. The vehicle was heavy, the acceleration completely different from a car. He'd expected to strike Olaf at speed, but his death was slow. The lorry struck him in the centre of the front grille. He fell onto the ground and was immediately hooked up by the lorry's undercarriage, his head banging on the asphalt as they moved across the car park.

His attackers were on the defensive now, heading for the safety of their vehicles. The car park was big enough for him to perform a wide turn, and as he swung the lorry round, a car drove into the car park from the motorway. When he saw what was happening, the driver slammed the car into reverse and roared back up the exit that he'd just come from.

Call the police, call the police! was all that Jack could think of as he swung the lorry around and headed for the vehicles abandoned in the middle of the parking area. He lined up the lorry, pushed down on the accelerator and aimed directly at the open door of one of the vans. He smashed straight into it, wrenching it from its hinges. It slid across the asphalt to land on the verge. He made a sharp turn, clipping a curb and dislodging Olaf's shredded body. He was herding them away from the vehicles, giving those bastards a taste of their own medicine.

To his side he saw Rosa breaking away with Lucy and an older man. Damn it, that was the guy Clive had been talking to in town that lunchtime. Jack did a double-take. It definitely was him. Clive! Had Clive landed them in this? Jesus, Clive was in his house right now, with his child.

Jack straightened out the lorry, aimed at the vehicles once again and smashed off another one of the open doors. The van pivoted awkwardly and this time the door stayed on its hinges. At the end of the car park he turned and took his foot off the gas. His two pursuers had seen what had happened to Olaf, they were cautious now, taking cover at the side of their damaged vans, anxious not to get caught out in the open. He could see Stefan, still bloodied from their earlier encounter.

Jack looked ahead. Lucy had been taken into the café and was sitting at one of the tables with Rosa at her side. Rosa was carrying a gun. The older man was speaking to somebody on a mobile device, looking agitated.

Jack leant over, moved the walkie-talkie closer and began to rev the engine. The two men took cover between the vans, expecting him to ram them. Good, if they thought he'd gone crazy it might serve him well. And, in a way, he had.

Jack thought through what he was going to do next. He made certain by checking the controls that he knew how to put the vehicle into reverse. He checked the café entrance, confirming one last time that it was set in light metal, rather than brick. Then he moved the lorry forward.

22

———

Sunday 03:11

Jack swung the lorry towards the two vans. He was bluffing, buying himself time. The two men took cover, waiting for an impact, but Jack had no intention of causing further damage to the vehicles.

He saw the moment that Rosa realised what was going on, as he careered away from the cluster of cars and directly towards the café window. Jack wanted them to think he was coming straight at them on some kind of suicide mission. As he neared the café, he turned the steering wheel to head straight for the entrance doors. He took his foot off the accelerator and clicked the button on the walkie-talkie.

—Remember India, Lucy. Remember the goat. Be ready.

He prayed that she would remember. They were much younger then, on holiday, deliriously in love. She'd been late for the tuk-tuk outside the hotel and the driver got so impatient he started off without her. She came out of the hotel door to see the tuk-tuk driving off. To Jack's amazement she ran alongside the vehicle, leapt onto its side, almost pulling it over in the process, and glided in next to Jack. It was a cross between Steven Seagal and Sebastian Coe, a remarkable manoeuvre, even more so because she'd had to leap over a goat to reach the moving vehicle. They'd laughed about that many times. He hoped she remembered, of course she would, it was one of their shared memories, a safe place they could return to whenever they seemed to be drawing apart.

The lorry crashed through the glass doorway. The flimsy metallic framework offered no resistance to the front of the vehicle, which fitted snuggly between the brick walls which had housed the entrance doors. Fragments of shattered glass covered the floor and the tables. Rosa and the older man cowered, giving Lucy the vital seconds that she needed.

She ran faster than he remembered her doing in India. She leapt from her seat, ran across three tables and jumped from the last to land on the step of the lorry cab. She clung on as he placed the vehicle into reverse and began to pull out of the café.

'Tuck yourself in!' he yelled at Lucy. Shit, he hadn't thought it through. She'd get caught on the walls. But with a superhuman effort, Lucy hauled herself up through the cabin window and launched herself into the lorry, her head resting on Calum's blood-soaked legs.

The lorry roared backwards, narrowly missing one of the men who'd finally dared to come out of hiding from the vehicles to their rear.

'Hold on!' Jack shouted. The lorry was going too fast. He had no idea how it would handle with such a long trailer at the back. He slammed on the brakes, moved the gears back into Drive, then headed directly for the exit.

'Are you okay? Luce, are you alright? I thought I'd killed you!'

Lucy sat up. She had seen so much death and violence that night that she barely registered the sight of Calum's body.

'I'm fine. Hell, Jack my head hurts. I think I was out cold for a few minutes in the car park, I whacked my head when we fell. That was some bloody rescue!'

For a moment, they didn't know whether to laugh or cry. She reached over, put her arms around his waist and rested her head on his shoulder. Jack did his best to keep his eyes on the road.

'Thank God you're okay. I thought I'd killed you. You fell from the cab just as I shot the gun. I really thought I'd got you.'

'They want your fingerprints, Jack. They need you alive. What on earth are you doing up there in Aberdeen?'

'They want my fingerprints? That must be to do with the biometric security project I'm working on. But it's only a working model. I have no idea why they want to access it.'

'Are we clear?' Lucy suddenly asked. 'Anybody behind us?'

'Not that I can see.'

'Pull over. I'll be fast.'

Jack stopped on the hard shoulder and Lucy opened the passenger door. Putting her whole body into it, she pushed Calum out so that he fell awkwardly onto the verge below.

'I'm sorry, Calum, but I'm not sharing this cab with a corpse. Let's get away from here.'

Jack did as he was told, the lorry jerking as he did his best to catch the feel of the pedals. It was all he could do to see what was ahead of them, the windscreen was badly damaged.

'I think we might have another problem,' he said. 'That man back there, the older one. Did you catch his name?'

'It's Franz. He's German I think. He's the guy in charge. He's the one pulling the strings. Why?'

'I've seen him before. In Aberdeen. He was talking to Clive—'

'Let's get off the motorway here,' she interrupted him. 'We need to shake them off.'

Lucy was right. They'd reached a slip road. There was no point staying on the motorway. Jack pulled the lorry off the carriageway.

She was studying him intently.

'What's this about Clive? You mean Clive knows that man back there? For Christ's sake, Jack. Are you telling me that Clive is behind all this?'

'I don't know, Lucy, I just don't know. But I got a pretty good look at that guy Franz, I'm certain it's him. And then with Matt Rackham involved too, it's got to be connected with what I'm doing in Aberdeen.'

'Damn it, Jack. We've left our son with that arsehole Clive!'

Jack drove in silence for a few moments, thinking it through. If Franz had been talking to Clive, maybe they were working together. Clive was a jerk, but really? How could he be involved with all of this?

'We've got to get Hamish away from him, Jack. For all we know, that's part of the plan. What if they're holding him hostage.'

Jack couldn't bear to consider the possibility. It was more than he cope with.

They were driving along an A-road now. They had to be nearing civilisation soon. Jack checked the mirrors and then he checked them again to make sure he'd seen correctly.

'How the hell can they know which route we took?' he shouted, punching his fist on the dashboard of the cab.

'They're not behind us are they? Please tell me they're not behind us already?'

'Unless somebody else is driving a van minus a drivers-side door at four o'clock in the morning, then, yes, they've found us. How the hell did they do that?'

'It's that bloody tracker of yours! I've told you before to stop broadcasting everything that you're doing. If they can find you on social media with that damn wristband on, they'll know exactly where we are. It might not be with pinpoint accuracy, but it's close enough to know that we turned off the motorway.'

Jack felt himself go sweaty. It made sense. They would have known that he was doing the run that weekend and that he would be wearing his GPS tracking device. And, if he really was involved in all of this, Clive might have told them about it. Is that how they knew where to find them in the woods. Had they been tracking him all day?

'Here, take it!' he snapped at Lucy, angry with himself for being so stupid. She had told him over and over again to watch his privacy settings. He'd taken no notice, he had thought it was harmless.

He looked in the wing mirror.

'They're holding back,' he said. 'I don't think they want us to know that they're there. Bit of a giveaway, the missing door.'

'I'm throwing this thing out of the window. I'm sick to death of it. If this is responsible for what's been happening, I'll ... I'll ...'

'You'll what, Lucy?'

Jack looked over at her.

'You'll leave me? Is that what's on the tip of your tongue?

Do you really want to have this conversation right now, Luce? I can think of better times.'

'Woah, be careful!'

In his anger, Jack had swung over to the other side of the road, quickly correcting himself.

'No, of course I don't mean that—'

'What do you mean, Luce? Because I've been treading on eggshells for weeks now, hoping you'll snap out of whatever it is that's bugging you. Look, I get it. We lost a child. Helen, we lost Helen. There's not a day goes by that I don't think about her. I could cry forever just thinking about her. But we have to go on, Lucy, for Hamish's sake. He deserves to have two parents who are present for him. He didn't die, you know – we still have one child who needs us.'

Lucy began to cry.

'I'm sorry. This isn't the time, I know.'

'What better time is there, Jack? We've been putting off this conversation for months. Look, I'm unhappy, but it's more than that, I've been depressed. I've even thought about killing myself. I feel so alone when you're in Aberdeen. I can't stop Hamish crying. He knows I don't love him.'

'You don't mean that,' Jack replied, more conciliatory now. 'I know you don't mean that. He knows you love him. He senses that you're unsure, it's that he picks upon. You mean the world to him, Luce, and you mean everything to me. I need you to—'

'Snap out of it? Is that what you were going to say, Jack? You want me to just snap out of it? Well, it's not quite as simple as that—'

'They're getting closer,' Jack interrupted, looking in his mirror. 'There are two of them now. The one at the back has his lights off, but I glimpsed him in the street lights.'

'Where are we?' Lucy asked. 'We can't be a million miles from home.'

'I reckon thirty maybe forty miles now,' Jack replied. 'We're about to come into a village. I've got an idea.'

'Whatever it is, you'd better make a start on it quickly, this road is narrowing and we're going to find ourselves stuck soon.'

Lucy held Jack's wristband in her hand. She was about to throw it out of the window when a sudden rush of sympathy for her husband made her place it back on her own wrist for safe-keeping.

'Can you turn this thing off?' she asked.

'It's in the privacy settings,' Jack answered. 'I'm not sure you can do it directly from the unit. Throw it away, I don't mind. If that thing is what's got us into this mess, then I'll throw it away myself.'

'I'll hang onto it a bit longer. They know where we are now and it might come in handy later. We might be able to use it to send them up the wrong track.'

'Good thinking, Luce. You always were the brains of the marriage.'

Jack was pleased they were no longer rowing, but his good mood didn't last long.

'Did you see that?' Lucy asked.

'What?'

'That's a low bridge sign back there. They're herding us, Jack. They must know this leads to a low bridge. That's why they're hanging back. They're waiting for us to get to it.'

'Here's the village now,' Jack said, passing an old and unloved phone box at the roadside. If he could only stop the lorry and use it to call the police. They'd been stupid to spend time arguing. They should have been marshalling their resources.

'Let's pull together what we have, Luce. The gun's on the shelf in front of you. Do you still have Erica's phone?'

Lucy reached into her pocket and placed it on the shelf.

'Mine's still knackered, I think, and Erica's mobile is pretty basic, but at least it doesn't have a PIN code. There's a walkie-talkie there too. Put it all in the middle, between our seats.'

As they drove through the length of the village, Jack sounded the horn of the lorry continuously. He'd wake up the inhabitants, some old git would surely complain to the police. The vehicles behind them fell back as the horn began to blare. They knew they'd got them cornered, but they were keeping their distance. The doorless van made them conspicuous.

Lights were being switched on in the houses by the road.

'What have we got?' Jack asked. He looked down at the pile of equipment they had gathered: walkie-talkie, gun, mobile phone and wristband.

'Jack, look out!'

There was the grating sound of metal against stone and an ear-splitting crunch as the roof of the lorry's cabin folded down towards their heads. They were thrown against the already shattered windscreen as the lorry came to an abrupt stop.

'What was that? What happened?' asked Jack, recovering himself quickly and picking a fragment of glass out of his cheek.

'We hit a rail bridge! Did you really not see it coming?'

'I wasn't concentrating, Luce. Are you okay? That was some jolt.'

'I've hurt my neck, but that's going to be the least of our problems. Can't you hear that noise?'

There was a rumble in the distance and the ground was vibrating.

'Damn, it's a train! It's about to go over the bridge.'

They inspected the debris to their sides. Lucy's side of the cab was jammed against the wall of the narrow stone bridge. There was very small space to the side of Jack, but the cab had been forced downward by the impact, pushing it to a few centimetres above their heads. They were completely wedged in with no idea at all what damage they'd done to the bridge. The train was almost upon them.

23

———

Sunday 04:12

Jack could hear a dull thudding noise coming from the rear of the lorry.

'They're coming for us through the back,' he said, more calmly than he felt.

'We have to get out of here. The only way they can get to us is from behind – or by crossing the track. Either way we need to get moving.'

She was right. Jack reached for the door handle. The pounding was getting louder. It wouldn't be long before they managed to break into the rear of the lorry.

The door didn't open.

'Shit, it's jammed!'

'Push it harder!' shouted Lucy. 'Come on, they'll be through soon.'

'It won't move, the roof has pushed down too far.'

The train was almost overhead now. There was a steady,

ominous rumbling as it neared the bridge. A couple of stones from the arch fell to the ground.

'Luce, I'm not sure how secure this bridge is. Look at that debris, the archway has been damaged in the impact'

'I think you're right, we'll be buried in here if it collapses. Come on, there's a way out of here!'

Lucy moved right up to Jack and started to kick at the damaged windscreen. Jack lay back a little on the seat to get a better angle, and they kicked together. At last it shattered enough for them to climb through it.

More stones fell from the arched roof of the tunnel, if too many became dislodged, the entire structure would cave in.

Jack went through first, placing a blanket that Lucy found at the back of the cab over the shattered glass. He moved through backwards, dropping to the ground in front of the jammed lorry, watching all the time for falling debris.

'They're almost through, Luce. And there's one heck of a crack in the bridge up there. Come on, we have to run! If they break through at the back, they'll be able to shoot at us.'

Jack shouted up the cab, urging Lucy to begin the awkward journey down to the ground. The stonework was beginning to rain down now, one strike from falling rubble and they could be knocked out cold.

There were gunshots from within the lorry's cargo area.

The train was directly overhead now. It was heavy and thunderous. Perhaps a freight train, Jack thought. Behind them, they could hear the noise of their attackers trying to break through at the back of the lorry. They had no option. They had to jump onto the train.

More stones shook loose from the bridge, one bouncing on the front of the lorry and narrowly missing Jack's leg.

'We have to move. Come on!'

Jack helped Lucy down from the cab then took her hand. They ran around to the front of the bridge. The steep bank to the left was heavily overgrown and securely fenced. At the top of the bank to the right was a hedge which adjoined the next-door churchyard.

'If we climb up the bank to the churchyard, we can get through that hedge and enter the railway that way,' said Lucy.

Jack started to clamber up pulling Lucy behind him. They didn't have time to go the long way round. Once the train had passed by there would be nothing between them and their pursuers.

'Fuck it, I'm going through!'

He dived into the mass of brambles, forcing his way through the branches and foliage. He tried to clear a path for Lucy, but there was no escaping the sharp thorns.

In seconds they were on the other side, standing next to the track as the front of the train started to slowly roll past, their only hope of getting out of there.

It was slow enough to jump on board. Bright yellow, it had the words Rail Grinding painted along the sides. It didn't appear to be grinding, Jack saw no sparks, it was just making its way slowly along the track. Jack selected a unit with a two-step ladder to the side and an enclosed area where they could safely take refuge. It was this or nothing, the train had almost passed now, they had to commit.

'You go first, Luce!'

'No, you go ahead. I'm going to need you to pull me up, I'm not sure I have the strength in my ankle.'

There was no time to argue. They could barely hear each other over the persistent rumble anyway. Jack began to run, he was aiming for the small red gate set between two carriages at the rear of the train on which a warning was emblazoned on a bright yellow safety sign *Authorized Personnel Only.*

The heavy railway sleepers were set into heaps of stones; they were hard on the feet, even with running shoes on. Jack jumped and swung towards the red gate. He missed and stumbled before recovering and trying again. This time he got it, he was on the train.

He turned towards Lucy, she'd dropped behind, hanging back when she'd thought Jack was about to fall.

'Come on Luce, run!'

He watched his wife's face as she grimaced through the pain, a flashing light on the carriage illuminating her discomfort every couple of seconds. Lucy picked up her pace and held out her hand to Jack. She'd have to outrun the train for a moment so that he could grab her and pull her up.

'Come on, Lucy. You can do it!'

He held out his arm as far as he could, hanging on to the protective railings at the end of the carriage.

The last carriage had now passed the bridge. Jack knew that it was now or never for Lucy. He knew what they would do to her if she didn't make it. They were ruthless.

She made a final desperate thrust forward, fighting through the pain of her injured ankle. Jack caught her hand and clasped it tightly pulling her up onto the train's decking. He slammed the small red gate firmly shut and held his wife as she gasped to catch her breath. They'd made it. They were safe. That narrow, gated area at the end of the carriage had provided sanctuary for the two fugitives.

'Make sure we're not being followed,' Lucy urged him, struggling to catch a full breath.

Jack helped his wife sit up against the side of the

carriage and looked back down the railway track. The fog had gone now and he could see clearly in the light of the moon.

'The other side,' Lucy signalled with her hand, 'check the other side too.'

He moved across the width of the train to look back down the tracks. There were three figures gathered at the top of the bridge. They were watching, even from that distance he could feel the tension.

Suddenly, a tall muscular figure appeared from behind the train. Jack watched in horror as he ran alongside the last carriage, and then leapt up towards the railings, just as he had done seconds earlier

They were no longer alone. There was no route they could use to make their escape through the carriages. They would have to climb up onto the roof.

24

———

Sunday 04:16

Jack moved fast, he'd seen the size of their pursuer. He was fit and strong, like the rest of them. Jack wouldn't stand a chance in a fight.

'Did you manage to bring anything from the lorry, Luce?'

He had to shout to be heard over the noise of the train.

She put her hand in her pocket. It was a small thing that Jack noticed, but because it was inside out Lucy had to reach awkwardly to retrieve the item. It was Erica's phone. What were they going to do, throw it at the guy? Lucy saw his disappointment as she placed the phone on the metal deck. She reached behind her into the elastic of her tracksuit bottoms. It was the gun. They could defend themselves at least.

Jack reached over and hugged his wife hard, relieved that she'd had the presence of mind to grab the most useful pieces of equipment from the lorry cab. He thought about the layout of the train. The man was two wagons behind them. It wouldn't take him long to move along the roof.

'We have to go up on top.'

'I don't think I can,' Lucy replied. 'My ankle hurts too much. Take the gun, you're going to have to fire at him. I'll use Erica's phone to try to raise the police. They want you alive, remember. They don't give a shit about me.'

She was right. If he went up on the roof he might wound or kill the man, but if Lucy went with him, she'd be shot without a second thought. He wished he'd paid more attention to all those films he'd watched so he could figure out how many rounds of ammunition he had left.

He decided to move across to the next carriage. It was enclosed by a metal frame which would serve as a ladder. He'd be able to get onto the roof from there. He tucked the gun into his waistband and began to pull himself up. Beneath him the sleepers flashed, creating a startling stroboscopic effect.

He scanned the top of the train before he pulled himself up. The man had got to the second carriage, he was almost upon them. Jack quickly moved to a squat. The train was swaying from side to side. They were entering a town, he could see streetlights. He thought it through, this had to be the rural line down to the city. It would take them close to home.

He put out his arms to balance and tentatively stood up. It was harder than it looked on the TV. Every so often the train would shake and nearly send him over the edge of the roof. His opponent was having the same difficulty too. He felt for the gun tucked into his waistband and pulled it out. The train shook again and he stumbled. He could see Lucy anxiously looking up, trying to see what was going on.

Jack levelled the gun at his pursuer. The man stopped

for a moment, he hadn't expected Jack to be armed. Their eyes met across the carriages, there was twenty metres between them. Jack recognised him. It was Johnson.

He stopped dead and examined Jack's face, working out what he was going to do next. Jack watched for a hand movement, but his opponent appeared to be unarmed. Jack raised the gun, aiming it as best as he could, and fired.

Johnson dropped to the roof of the carriage, and for a moment Jack thought he'd hit him, but he was only protecting himself, lying flat and making himself less of a target. Jack raised the gun again and fired a second time, but the train lurched making him stumble and causing the shot to go wildly into the air. Johnson leapt to his feet and moved forward another five metres before ducking down again as Jack, completely bungling his timing, fired again, the bullet ricocheting off the metal of the next carriage.

He suddenly became aware of Lucy frantically waving at him, pointing above his head. What was it? What was she trying to signal to him? He glanced up to see a flash, then another.

Johnson was waiting to make another move. He was almost at the end of the second carriage, he'd be right over Lucy's head soon. Could she shoot him through the canopy if he threw her the gun? Jack wondered how many bullets he had left. How many had he wasted, two ... three? He'd lost count. He considered his options. He decided he would move up the carriages to lure Johnson away from Lucy.

Jack levelled the gun, wise to the motion of the train by now. He waited for it to shake, he was ready for it and steadied himself. He aimed directly at Johnson and pulled the trigger. The gun clicked. Jack tried again. Johnson was getting back up on his feet, a contemptuous smirk on his face.

Below him Lucy was still gesticulating at him, increasingly frustrated at his failure to understand her. Something whizzed over his head. Another flash. At last he understood.

It was just the two of them now, a fight without weapons on the roof of a moving train.

They were moving into the city. Jack caught sight of the floodlit cathedral, a welcome landmark. The train was slowing, he didn't have much time. He looked at Johnson and placed his gun on the roof of the carriage. Jack counted the flashes overhead, getting his timing right. Johnson looked him dead between the eyes, calculating his move. Slowly Jack stepped backwards, giving his opponent just enough clearance to make his jump. There was a shake of the train, both men steadied themselves, and then Johnson started to run before leaping up high to clear the gap between the wagons. Jack saw the spray of blood and then the flash of electricity.

Johnson had leapt up directly into the path of one of the heavy frames which carried the electrified cables. That's what Lucy had been shouting at him. As Johnson had made his jump, his head had crashed into the structure, instantly crushing his skull. His body was thrown into the air, entangled in the cables which carried the power for the electrified lines. If he wasn't dead by the time he hit the solid metal frame, there would have been no doubt about it after what was left of his body fried on the 25,000-volt cable over their heads.

25

———————

Sunday 04:47

Trembling, Jack sank to the carriage roof before his legs gave way under him. The train was slowing. He wasn't familiar with this approach to the station, but he could see they were moving into the city centre. Shakily, he made his way down the metal frame and back to Lucy. She hugged him, hard. They didn't speak. They both had tears running down their faces.

'What do we do now?' she asked.

'We've got to call the police.'

'I want to ring home first. I want to see what that shit Clive is up to. The bastard has our child!' It was getting light. She looked at Erica's phone. It was nearly five o'clock. 'Hamish will probably be awake already. There's something that's been bothering me about this ...'

Lucy dialled the home phone number.

The phone rang until it switched to answer phone. Lucy dialled straight in again. Again it switched through to Lucy's bland message, accompanied by the sound of Hamish wailing in the background.

Hi, we can't take your call at the moment, please leave a message.

'They must still be sleeping,' Lucy said, disappointed.

The train had stopped alongside a platform. There were no passengers around, and apart from the cooing of the pigeons, the station was eerily quiet. There was a taste of engine fumes in the air, Jack hadn't noticed that while they'd been moving.

'Come on, Lucy. We need to get off this train and call the police.'

Jack opened the small red safety gate and stepped out onto the platform. Erica's phone started to vibrate in Lucy's hand. The train was still idling, but now it had stopped moving they could talk at normal levels again.

'Hello,' said Lucy, expecting to hear Sophie's voice returning her call. It wasn't Sophie. It was the woman in the cemetery. She recognised the voice. She didn't beat around the bush.

'Is your husband with you? Yes, I can see that he is. We've been tracking you.'

The German accent seemed more pronounced over the phone.

'Yes, I'm here,' Jack said, his heart beating fast.

'Mr Dawson, you have caused us a lot of trouble this evening. This is what is going to happen—'

'Have you got Hamish there?' Lucy interrupted. 'Is he alright? Is he safe?'

The woman ignored her.

'Mr Dawson, please quieten your wife. My colleagues and I are getting onto a private plane at 6.30am, that's in just over one hour's time. It will take you a maximum of thirty minutes to drive to your house, where I will require you to place three fingerprints onto an electronic device. Once you have done that, we will be on our way. If we miss our take-off window at the airport, we will be extremely angry.'

Jack could hear a sniffing in the background. It must be Sophie. And there he was, Hamish, happy and gurgling, as if nothing was wrong.

'What's this all about?' Jack asked. 'Whatever you're doing, is it really worth all of this?'

'Jack, I'm sorry! I didn't know it would turn out like this. I only—'

It was Clive's voice. There was a gunshot. Then silence.

'Oh my God! Clive? Sophie? What was that?'

'Half an hour, Mr Dawson. No police. Not unless you want to be visiting another child's grave with your wife.'

The call ended.

The last thing that Jack heard was Sophie screaming.

26

––––––––

Sunday 04:56

'Oh my God! Oh my God!'

Lucy said the words over and over again. If she was pale before, now she was ashen.

'What happened, Jack? What did they do? Did they kill somebody?'

Jack wanted to scream. He'd had enough. He didn't know if he had the energy to see it through, but they had his child – what could he do? It was as they'd thought. It was his fingerprints they were after. No wonder they needed him alive. He knew that much at least, the fingers had to be attached to a living person.

The driver was leaving the train, walking over to a colleague who'd come out of a small office along the platform.

Jack focused, he knew that they had to act fast if any of them were getting out of this hell.

'Luce, I want you to distract those two guys. Walk over to

them and I'm going to get something from the train.'

Lucy didn't need to do much distracting. When the men saw the state she was in they rushed towards her to help. Jack darted up into the cab and quickly rummaged around for a first aid kit. There was one hanging on the wall. He tore it off, picked up a wallet that was lying on the dashboard, and jumped back onto the platform. He grabbed Lucy's hand and they ran to the footbridge which crossed the line.

'I need to take her to hospital!' he shouted. 'Thanks for your help.'

'Give me my wristband,' Jack said, working it off Lucy's wrist as she stretched it out towards him. 'Follow me – don't look behind you.'

They passed the closed ticket office and walked past the newsagent's. Its shutter was halfway down and he could hear voices inside. They must be sorting the papers, the world was waking up. Outside the station entrance, there was a blue van parked with its engine running. The driver was nowhere to be seen.

Jack worked it out quickly. The Sunday papers and milk were being delivered and the driver was chatting to the shopkeeper. He had no idea that his vehicle was about to be stolen. It was better than Jack had hoped. He walked quickly over to the taxi drivers who were huddled around the window of one of the vehicles, sharing a joke.

'Sorry to disturb you,' he interrupted, 'but I need to get this wallet back to its owner at the hospital. Here's a twenty-pound note for the fare, you can keep the change. It's for Dr Neil Patel – can you leave it at reception for him?'

The other drivers moved away. Jack followed the driver to his vehicle and threw his wristband into the back of the car as he was climbing in. Those bastards would still be tracking them. Once he got home he'd tell them that Lucy had gone to the hospital. That should give her and Sophie a chance to get Hamish out safely.

'You know there's no way out of this now,' Lucy said. 'Not if they're in the house. Not if they have Hamie. You know they're going to kill us all, don't you? No one is getting out of this. They're going to do whatever it is they want to do with your fingerprints, and then they'll kill us all. You do understand that, right?'

'Of course I do, but I'm not going without a fight. They can have my fingerprints, I don't care what they do to me, but I refuse to give up another child and I won't let them hurt you. There was nothing we could to save Helen, but we can save Hamie. And we're going to have to do it together. Okay?'

Lucy looked deep into her husband's eyes and saw reflected back a man who loved her, who would risk his life for her. For them. Her and Hamish.

She'd do it. She and Jack together, they'd work as a team and get their child out of there.

'Okay,' she said. 'Let's do it. What's the plan?'

'Get in the passenger seat.' Jack nodded towards the delivery van. 'Some people are going to have to make do without a Sunday paper this week.'

27

———————

They barely spoke throughout the drive. It was a familiar route for Jack, it was his way home. Usually he felt excited to be home at last, but also anxious. What state would Lucy be in when he got there? Would Hamish be crying? But now all he could think about was how they would get out of there alive.

As they entered the outskirts of the village, it was quiet, most people were still in bed. If things had gone to plan, they should have been home a couple of hours ago, quietly entering the house via the back door and sleeping on the made-up sofa bed in the snug at the back until Hamish stirred. They'd have enjoyed a fry-up when everybody was awake and then Clive and Sophie would have gone their separate ways.

Lucy could take the spare key from the false stone next to the sundial and creep through the back door to go to get Hamish. Meanwhile, he'd go in by the front door to distract the woman. Her voice had been familiar. Did he know her? He suddenly realised who she was. He'd met her in Aberdeen, it was Anna.

Jack pulled the van onto the verge a couple of hundred metres away from the house leaving the keys in the ignition.

'Okay, Lucy. All you have to do is to go through the back door and find Hamish. Once you've got him, take him to the van and drive. It doesn't matter where you go, just get away.'

'What about you? What about Clive and Sophie?'

'We'll have to take our chances – that's if Clive is still okay.'

Jack paused a moment. How had it come to this in such a short time? It seemed crazy to think that his colleague – his friend – might have been shot dead. Things had happened that night that were beyond belief.

He was aware of a persistent mechanical sound in the distance. It was getting louder.

'What's the time?'

Lucy checked the screen on Erica's phone.

'It's nearing 6 o'clock. You need to get in there.'

The noise was loud now and directly overhead.

'It's a helicopter!' Jack craned his neck to look through the van window. 'Is it the police?'

Lucy stepped out of the van and Jack followed her, just in time to see it move behind the trees.

'Not police, at least I don't think so,' she said.

'They've landed in the field behind the house. It'll be the rest of them that we left behind at the railway bridge, that's how they're getting to the airport. The buggers have it all planned out, they must have had that helicopter hidden near the woods.'

'You need to go, Jack.'

'No heroics,' he replied, walking over to her. 'Get Hamie out of there and stay safe. Let me take care of the rest.'

He moved towards Lucy and she put her arms around him, pulling him in tight.

'I love you, Jack. I'm sorry things have been so shit recently.'

'I know, I know,' Jack replied. 'It's okay, we'll work this out. Together, we'll sort this.'

He kissed her and pulled slowly away, not wanting the moment to end. It struck him for a moment that this might be the last time he got to hold his wife. No, he wouldn't let that happen.

Lucy nodded, squeezed Jack's hand, then walked across the verge into the trees that lined the road. She would use them for cover right up to their garden, then sneak up to the back door. She had to pray that Hamish would be in his bedroom or, better still, in the snug.

Jack checked that he'd left the keys in the van. There would be no car seat for Hamish on his next journey.

He began to walk along the road. He could hear the helicopter idling. Would the local population assume it was some rich guy flying overhead or perhaps a police helicopter? As he approached the house, he saw three cars outside. Their own was there and one was Clive's. The other was large and black, it probably belonged Anna.

He walked up to the front door, his mouth dry, his heart beating fast, terrified at what he was going to find there.

They were ready for him.

28

'At last, Mr Dawson. This could have been a lot easier if you'd played nice. Anna Reichmann, by the way. We've met already, you'll recall.'

Jack heard footsteps on the gravel. Someone was walking around the side of the house. It was the bearded man who'd been talking to Clive in Aberdeen.

'Hello, Franz. Perfect timing,' she said.

He didn't reply. Instead he opened the black leather briefcase he was carrying and pulled out a laptop. It was like nothing Jack had seen before, it wasn't an off-the-shelf model, this was bespoke.

'Your wife seems to have gone elsewhere. We've been monitoring that tracker of yours. The hospital? I hope she knows to keep her mouth shut.'

'She does,' Jack replied. 'She was in no state to come to the house. She knows not to say anything.'

'You've secured the line?' Franz asked.

Anna nodded.

'I dialled in a few weeks ago. It's all sorted.'

'Okay, Mr Dawson. Let's do this.'

There was a strong smell of petrol moving through the house. Where was it coming from? Fumes from the helicopter perhaps.

Jack was ushered into the sitting room. That was good, he could try to keep them contained while Lucy sneaked in the back. Where was Hamish? The first thing that he noticed was a splash of blood against the wall.

He stopped dead. Anna pushed him forward.

Stefan was already standing in the room. His face was bruised and his right eye purple and swollen. He tensed and snarled, recalling how Jack had kicked him earlier. He took his arm and gave it a sharp twist, eager to get his own back on this runt of a man. He pushed him into a chair in front of the spattered blood. Was this where Clive had been executed?

'How long do we have now, Franz?'

The older man looked at his watch. It was an expensive one, it was funny how Jack noticed that in spite of everything.

'And Rosa?'

Franz looked directly into Anna's eyes and gave a small nod.

'And Rosa too,' he said.

Whatever had passed between them, Anna knew exactly what he meant.

'Let's get this done,' he said.

From inside his jacket, he drew out a small handgun and shot Stefan directly between the eyes, unflinching as he pulled the trigger. The big man dropped heavily to the ground. Jack gasped. It was a cull. If they were killing their own, what chance did he have?

Anna had been tapping away at the laptop and now held it out to Franz. Franz turned it around so that the screen was facing Jack. He recognised this. It was the fingerprint access screen that he used for work.

'What's this all about?' he asked. 'What can you possibly want with this? It's inconsequential.'

'You might think that, Mr Dawson, but your colleague Matt Rackham has had you working on a project of slightly more importance than you might believe. Now, please, your fingerprints.'

'And what happens when I touch that screen? You kill me anyway?'

'Yes, Mr Dawson. You don't get out of this one, but I'm sure you've worked that out already. Have you any idea how much a cure for Alzheimer's is worth globally? Probably not, you just write code. It's worth losing a few lives for, let's put it that way.'

'And what about my baby? Where's Hamish – and Clive and Sophie?'

'Your friend is dead. Although he was never your friend. Do you know how much he sold you out for? Fifty thousand euros. That's how broke he was. If you want something to remember him by, don't redecorate in here.'

Jack was going into shock. He couldn't move, a paralysis had gripped his body.

'And if I don't give you my fingerprints?'

'It makes no difference, Mr Dawson. We shoot you anyway. We can get your prints before you're brain dead. You know how these things work.'

Jack vomited onto the sofa. Strangely, it gave him the kick he needed. He wiped the side of his mouth and eyed

Stefan's gun. When Franz had shot him, the dead man's weapon had flown out of his hand, coming to rest on the rug at the far side of the sitting room.

Anna wasn't carrying a weapon or, at least not one that Jack could see. He calculated that if he could disable Franz in some way and make a run for the gun, he might at least stand some chance of fighting back.

With Franz now leaning over him, the laptop in his right hand, the gun in his left, Jack scooped his hand into the pool of vomit and threw it at Franz's face.

29

———

Sunday 05:49

'Only another half-hour, only another half-hour,' Lucy chanted to herself, forcing her mind off the pain and driving her body forward. She was exhausted, completely spent. But everything would play out in a matter of minutes now. If she could get Hamish out unharmed, if Jack could escape, it would all be over. She wanted to lie down and sleep for a week.

The trees which bordered the garden were beginning to thin. She needed to stay alert. Lights were on in the house – in the living room, and there was a dim light on in Hamish's bedroom. It was his night-light. That was bad news, she'd hoped they'd put him down in the snug. He often slept there at night.

Lucy scanned the rear of the garden. It backed onto fields. She could hear the sound of a helicopter idling. She needed to stay alert. How many of them were around?

She hopped over the three-bar fence which bordered

their garden and ran across the vegetable patch to the cover of the garden shed. There was movement at the back door. Damn, that was her only way of getting in. She waited and watched. She could see a figure carrying a large metal container into the house through the open door.

Lucy watched and waited. It was one person on their own. She had no time, she had to get Hamish. She grabbed Jack's axe from the low log store next to the woodpile behind the shed. At least she'd look threatening, even if she didn't feel it. She waited for the figure to turn their back and ran across to the small outhouse where she'd be able to see what was going on.

It was Rosa. The bitch was indestructible. She had already taken one can inside the house and Lucy watched as she took the cap off the second and walked in with it.

Lucy followed, petrol fumes sweeping over her as she stepped into the house. The bastards were going to burn them down. She looked ahead, expecting to see Rosa emptying the contents of the can along the hallway and up the stairs. Instead, she saw her listening at the door of the living room. Then all hell was unleashed.

30

Sunday 05:52

Franz was caught completely unawares. He recoiled. Jack seized his chance, darting across the room towards the gun.

While Franz was retching and wiping his face, Anna was fumbling in her pocket. Jack assumed she was reaching for a weapon. The laptop tumbled to the floor. Jack grasped Stefan's gun and turned to point it at them. Suddenly Rosa walked into the room. Startled, he fired the gun too soon, hitting one of the ceiling lights and spraying Franz and Anna with fragments of glass.

To his horror, as he was about to fire the gun a second time, Lucy ran into the room, the kindling axe raised above her head. She lunged at Rosa, who in a flash spun Anna in front of her. Jack fired and the bullet grazed Rosa's leg, while Lucy's axe drove deep into Anna's forehead. She dropped to the floor, her eyes wide open, her body convulsing in shock.

Franz had now recovered and was clutching his gun,

trying to work out who was the greater threat, Jack, Rosa or Lucy.

'They're going to burn the house down!' Lucy screamed.

'Shut the fuck up, bitch,' said Rosa, striking her across the face. Lucy fell to the floor.

Jack fired again and the room was silent. Franz swung around and shouted to Rosa.

'You need to get me out of here.'

'And what then, you little shit. You have me killed as soon as we land at the airport? No, that's not happening.'

'Where's the baby?' Jack demanded.

Rosa nodded towards the stairs.

'In his bedroom along with that stupid cow of a babysitter. I had to shut her up, she makes a lot of noise.'

There was some kind of liquid pooling behind Rosa. Had someone pissed themselves in the panic? It was only when he saw Rosa's hand move to her pocket that Jack worked out what was going on. She was so fast.

As her left hand moved to her pocket, Rosa ripped the axe out of Anna's split face with her right. She hurled it at Jack. As he recoiled, Rosa flicked the flint on the lighter that she'd been carrying in her pocket and threw it to the ground. The axe flew past Jack's face and fell to the floor. There was a roar as flames leapt up along the hallway and straight into the back of the house.

'Oh Jesus – Hamish!' Lucy cried, still recovering from Rosa's violent blow.

Rosa kicked her in the face, then stood on her hand inches away from the fire.

'Franz, get this bastard's fingerprints and let's get out of here. You won't want to fuck your wife any more once she's been thrown in the fire, Mr Dawson, so I suggest you get on with it.'

Franz pointed the gun at Lucy.

'I'll be needing those fingerprints, Mr Dawson.'

Lucy was screaming as the flames began to lick around her hand. Rosa pushed down harder with her foot.

'Okay, okay,' Jack said, 'I'll give you the fingerprints, but you go then, alright? You leave us?'

Franz and Rosa looked at each other. It was a reluctant collusion, but they nodded. There was no way they were getting out of that house alive, but they needed his compliance now. Jack held his gun out, covering both Rosa and Franz. It was a stalemate. Both sides had weapons, Jack wanted to live, they needed his fingerprints.

'For fuck's sake, get off her hand!' Jack shouted. Rosa didn't move.

'The fingerprints.'

Jack activated the panel on the laptop which had fallen to the ground. It fired up, recognising his prints, and Franz rushed over to retrieve the machine. Lucy was shrieking with pain, the flesh on her arm raw with the heat of the fire.

Franz tapped some buttons on the keyboard, made sure that he'd got what he'd come for, and slammed down the lid.

'Let's get out of here!' he shouted.

Rosa rushed over to one of the windows, their exit now hazardous from the flames. She opened it, leapt onto the windowsill and climbed out. Franz watched Jack to make sure he didn't make a move against them.

'Here, give me the gun.'

Franz hesitated for a moment before passing it to her. He didn't have a choice, Rosa would need to cover him to make sure that Jack didn't shoot. He began to scramble through the window.

'Here, take this.' He handed the laptop to Rosa.

Jack had rushed to Lucy who was screaming with pain. The fire was increasing in intensity, it would soon have hold of the entire house.

Then, a gunshot. Jack thought he'd pulled the trigger of his own weapon by mistake, but it wasn't him. He looked towards Franz who was perched on the windowsill, then gasped as he dropped back into the sitting room, dead.

Rosa looked back into the room, pointing the gun at Jack.

'You think I can't fly a chopper, you fucker?' she hissed, and then was gone, running to the field at the back of the house towards the helicopter.

'The baby,' Lucy pleaded. 'We have to get to Hamish.'

'Help me with the rug!' Jack shouted.

In spite of the pain of her burned hand, Lucy managed to pick up one end. They worked together to beat back the flames in the living room and then threw it over the first three stairs where the fire had begun to take hold.

They ran upstairs, the heat from below was ferocious. Jack burst into Hamish's room. Sophie was sitting on the floor next to the cot, her face bloody and bruised. Her wrists and ankles were bound with parcel tape, her mouth taped up too. Jack quickly released her using some scissors which were lying on the chest of drawers.

'Where's Hamie?' Lucy screamed, rushing between the bedrooms. 'Where is he?'

'They've taken him,' Sophie gasped.

'Where? Jesus, where have they taken him?' asked Jack.

'They took him when the helicopter came. Oh God, Jack. They shot Clive. They just shot him. What the fuck is going on?'

Jack didn't reply. Instead he ran into the spare room and pulled the mattress off the bed. He opened the window on the landing and heaved it through. It dropped to the ground beneath.

'I'll go first, Lucy, and you and Sophie follow. Okay?'

She nodded at him. Jack threw the gun out of the window then jumped up onto the windowsill, letting himself down slowly by holding onto the sill, and then dropping onto the mattress.

Behind him the helicopter blades were speeding up. He picked up his gun and ran towards the back of the garden. He jumped straight over the fence to see Rosa about to tip Hamish's carrycot out of the chopper. He sprinted towards her, having one last shot at her as he ran.

She looked at him and deliberately dropped the carrycot onto the ground. She slid over into the pilot's seat. Jack jumped up to the open window slamming her face with the butt of his gun. He ducked as he felt the downward force of the blades. He leant into the cockpit, feeling around for the ignition. He found the key, pulled it out and threw it into the grass. He rushed towards Hamish, his heart pounding in his chest. His son couldn't be seen, his carrycot had fallen on top of him.

It didn't take Rosa long to recover. She jumped out of the helicopter and leapt onto Jack's back, her hands clasped around his neck. She was so strong. He couldn't breathe, he couldn't throw her off. She wouldn't let go. He dropped the gun and thrashed around, desperate to free himself of her grip. He could feel the downward pressure of the blades, but they were slowing now that the engine had been turned off.

He had one last chance, one final opportunity to finish this damn woman off for good. He moved away from Hamish towards the outer reaches of the blades. Still she squeezed, his windpipe was being crushed. He was fading now, there wasn't long left. With one last almighty effort, he thrust upwards. As they slowed, the outer tips of the blades had begun to drop lower. It was enough. With that final push, Rosa moved directly into their path, slicing off the top of her head before she even realised what was happening.

31

———

Two Months Later

'How are you doing?' Jack asked. 'Have you got a stitch?'

'Better than I thought,' Lucy replied. 'My ankle's still sore but I can run on it.'

She smiled at him. She'd thanked him over a hundred times already for what he'd done that night. He'd saved their baby.

Hamish gurgled in the buggy as if he sensed they were thinking about him.

'I don't know why we never thought about doing this before,' she continued. 'These three-wheeled buggies are brilliant. Hamish and I could have been out running all the time when you were away.'

They were nearing the house. Jack could see the bright red of the *Sold* sign. He'd begun to think that they'd never see one of those, but after the fire the site had been levelled for safety. Jack and Lucy were living in the garden, in a caravan, while the insurance got sorted out.

A builder had called in speculatively one day while they were eating lunch. Would they sell it as a building plot? he'd asked. He could get six retirement houses on that land.

It was a good deal, strong enough to get them out of there and settle their debts. It would be cheaper in the town, they'd get a lot more for their money. They were done with the countryside and rural living.

What happened that night hit them hard. Several times they'd given themselves up for dead, but they'd made it through. They'd survived because they'd worked together. They did it. The two of them.

Clive had set him up. He'd been working with Matt Rackham. The bastards had been using Jack's project as a Trojan horse. While Jack thought he was working on some other project, Matt Rackham was concealing highly confidential research data in the code and Clive was making deals with some German contacts who could sell valuable information stored inside the code to some shady operation in Israel. It was way beyond him, but those treacherous fuckers had got him involved without a thought for his family or his welfare.

In his more uncharitable moments, Jack thought they'd got what they deserved. It was Sophie he felt sorry for though. Clive had been spinning her some bullshit yarn when he was up to his ears in debt. Yes, Clive really was a shit.

As they drew up to the house, Jack could see that Maxine was waiting for them, sitting on the caravan step.

Lucy waved and Hamish giggled when he saw who it was.

It reminded Jack of the way he'd laughed when he gingerly moved the carrycot to see if his baby son had been hurt in the fall from the helicopter. Not a scratch! Hamish was completely oblivious, thinking that his dad was playing hide-and-seek with him.

'Is that you off then?' Lucy asked.

'Yes, I'm all packed and ready to go. I'm going to miss you all. And Hamish. Send me photos on Facebook, won't you?'

'Thanks so much for everything you've done, Maxine,' Jack said. 'We really appreciate it.'

'When do you start your new job?' Maxine asked him.

'Two more weeks,' he answered. 'After Lucy has finished the treatment on her hand.'

He looked down at the bandages. No lasting damage, thank God. Lucy's hand would heal, they'd said, with only a small amount of scarring.

'I've got something for you – in the caravan,' Lucy said, opening the door and stepping inside.

She came out with a card and a present.

'It's a small gift to get you underway at university. I hope you like it.'

Maxine hugged her and looked into Lucy's face, concerned.

'You are sure?' Maxine asked. 'You're certain that you're going to be okay now?'

Lucy looked at Hamish, then at Jack. She took her husband's hand and squeezed it.

'It's lovely that you asked,' she said, tears forming in her eyes. 'But I'm better now, thank you. We're better. Everything is good again. Things are going to work out for all of us.'

If you enjoyed this book, you'll love the Morecambe Bay series of psychological thrillers. Nine books and non-stop suspense. Available in paperback and e-book formats.

AUTHOR NOTES

I wrote Dead of Night immediately after completing the Don't Tell Meg trilogy.

I wanted to write a standalone thriller without a cliffhanger ending - one which was completely self-contained.

Often when I write my books I start out with a powerful image and take it from there.

I loved the idea of driving a car through dense woodland in the dead of night and then out of nowhere striking something - or someone - and having to get out into that darkness and find out what damage you've just done.

And then, to add to the tension, you have a bunch of people with guns roll up in a car and start taking shots at you.

I can't remember when I had the idea but I loved it straight away and had to base a book around that.

As with most of the characters in my books, Jack and Lucy start the story in a difficult place.

They have lost one of their children, they are badly in

debt and Jack has had to take a job far away from home in order to keep the money coming in.

Lucy is still depressed after the loss of a child, yet she still has her twin to care for, even though she's not sure that she even loves Hamish.

She finds herself isolated in the middle of nowhere with Jack away all week and she's going quietly mad.

This book was always intended to be a roller coaster of a ride but I do hope that it has strong emotional element to it, in that Jack and Lucy have a lot to resolve in their marriage throughout this book.

Originally the babysitter Maxine was going to be a baddie, but I decided to give the poor girl a break and let her go to university and improve her lot in life.

As I wrote the story it became obvious to me that Clive was the one who was most likely to betray a friend and although he's not as evil as some of the people who are chasing Jack and Lucy through the woods, he is a bit of a treacherous man and finally gets his comeuppance.

The character of Callum was fun to write even though the poor guy comes to a sticky end.

I decided that he couldn't stay in the book for too long because international readers might find his way of speaking difficult to follow for any prolonged period of time.

I loved writing the character of Rosa as she's a real kick ass woman and is more sensible that all of the guys put together.

She's the last one standing at the end of the book and it was almost a shame to finish her off in the way that I did, but at least she got a really dramatic ending.

I always bring lots of personal influences into my books and I'll let you know a few of them that I applied in this story.

When my wife and I moved to Cumbria, we lived in a ridiculously remote house in the middle of nowhere.

It was so isolated that my wife insisted we buy a second car as we had two very young children at the time and she refused to be stuck in the house all day.

This is what I based Lucy's experiences on, only Lucy didn't have a second car to help her escape from that rural isolation.

Although I don't run as much as I'd like, I've had some experience of taking part in running events and of jogging along country lanes just like Jack and Lucy.

Maxine is based on our experiences of a girl who did some babysitting for us when our children were young and she was a great babysitter too, which is one of the reasons I decided that her character should get a break and not end up as one of the casualties of this story.

Although my thrillers are never meant to be funny, I do hope that you spot the occasional laugh in the stories and there was one scene that I just couldn't resist writing in Dead of Night.

It's the scene at the service station in the kitchen when one of the thugs ends up with flour and beaten eggs on his head - I just couldn't resist having him thrust into a deep fat fryer, it was too good dramatic opportunity to miss.

Although I'm quite vague about the geography of this book, I know exactly where most of the action happens in this story.

For instance, the bridge through which Jack is unable to drive the lorry is located in a Cumbrian village where we once lived.

I modelled the entire situation of the bridge in that village, right down to scrambling up at the side through the churchyard to reach the railway line.

I was extremely fortunate whilst writing this book to be able to get a look inside a lorry so that the scenes in which Jack is trying to drive away are as realistic as possible.

A local driving school was recruiting in the city centre and had driven a lorry into the pedestrianised area in the hope of recruiting new trainee drivers.

The gentleman who was in charge of the display allowed me to climb on board and take lots of photographs and the timing couldn't have been better for this book.

I wanted to know if somebody like me, who's never driven a lorry before, would be able to jump straight into a lorry cab and start driving, albeit badly.

The gentleman that I spoke to had been driving lorries for years and assured me that although you'd probably make a bit of a mess of it, you could just jump into a cab and start driving.

One of the things I hadn't realised beforehand is that lorries are fitted with automatic gearboxes, so that instantly makes the whole process easier.

If you liked this story and want to stay in touch, I'd be delighted if you registered for my email updates at https://paulteague.net/thrillers, as that's where I share news of what I'm writing and tell you about any reader discounts and freebies that are available.

Paul Teague

ONE LAST CHANCE PREVIEW

Prologue

It took three swipes of the axe to hack off his finger. At last they realised this was no joke. They'd seen Sebastian's advertising antics on TV and knew that he was capable of pulling the most elaborate of stunts. Right up to the moment the axe had struck and they'd heard the sickening crunch of bone and sinew, they'd been convinced that the look of deadly seriousness on Sebastian's face would melt into a huge smile, the menacing group of men who'd burst into the room would begin to laugh, and it would all be over.

Jerry fell to the ground. He'd passed out from the shock. His livelihood would be ruined. They must have known who he was to target him so mercilessly. The leader of the gang, Baptiste, watched impassively as he slumped to the floor, his blood spilling crimson onto the cream carpet. He pulled the Rolex off Jerry's wrist.

'Half a million dollars,' he said, his accent betraying a hint of French. He held up the watch to the light ignoring the blood that was spattered along the wristband. 'I'd say that was worth losing a finger for, wouldn't you? Now, your jewellery please. I don't want to have to do any more damage to this lovely carpet. Mr Helix will be claiming on his accidental damage policy as it is. Let's not do anything hasty to further erode his enormous fortune.'

Without making a sound, the guests quickly followed his orders placing their jewellery in plastic bags. Watching from the safety of the doorway, Matt reckoned there must be a million pounds worth in one bag alone. He and Clare were out of their depth. They'd never fit in with these people. And now look at the danger he'd placed her in. He watched as one of the men – a skinny, unkempt lout called Leon, who looked like he needed a good bath – moved right up close to her, sweeping her long hair back across her shoulders, checking for anything which might be worth taking.

'Nothing on this one,' he shouted over to his boss. 'Just a wedding ring.'

Baptiste walked over, placing his hands on Clare's hips and running them slowly and threateningly up her waist.

'Interesting. Here is our cuckoo in the nest.'

'You leave her alone!' Sebastian shouted. Before he had time to speak again, a third man with a livid scar across his face had smashed his fist into the millionaire's chest, shutting him down instantly and leaving him writhing on the floor. Baptiste glared at the scarred man angrily, but said nothing.

Matt could see the guests flinching as they watched their host lying helpless and in pain. Their money counted for nothing here. It gave them no clout and no privilege. They were at the mercy of a bunch of pirates, at sea, in a place where nobody would be able to come and save them.

'Which one is your husband?' asked the man with the scarred face.

'Which of these snivelling little shits are you married to? I'm guessing it's his money that gets you horny, not his stunning good looks ... not looking at the state of this lot anyway. What you need is a real man, someone who knows what a woman wants.'

He was right up close to her now. Matt held himself back with every last force of will that he could muster. He would kill that man. He would kill his grinning companions. And then he would return home with his wife, they'd continue living their crappy little lives, and he'd play no part in whatever it was that Sebastian Helix had got planned for him.

'Which one is your husband?' the man barked at her once again. Clare was crying now. There was no answer she could give to save Matt. Whatever she said, they'd be bound to find him. They knew how many people were in that place and there was no getting off, not until the storm died down. It would only be a matter of time before they located him.

Matt took a last look at his wife from the safety of the entrance to the bar area. Across the room he could see a man brandishing a machine gun, threatening the cowering chef and catering team, who were on their knees lined up against the far wall. Carefully, he let the swing door shut behind him, moved to the end of the bar and then headed off along the gently curved corridor.

They would come for him, of course. It didn't take a genius to work out that there was an extra table setting. They'd already figured out that Clare didn't belong. He knew that they were dispensable. They had nothing to offer: no bank account filled to the brim, no jewellery to sell on the black market.

Matt paused by the tray of drinks which had been left half-finished on the bar. He picked up the knife that the barman had been using to chop a lemon for a G&T, before he'd been bludgeoned and left to die on the floor. It was all he had for protection.

Behind him he heard a cry. It was Clare. The bastards. Frustration and helplessness seared through his body. He loved his wife more than anything. All he cared about was their life together. The deal with Sebastian Helix was meaningless in comparison. First he had to save his wife and then he was going to tell Helix and that bloody assistant of his where they could stick their investment money.

One Last Chance is available as a paperback or e-book.

ALSO BY PAUL J. TEAGUE

Morecambe Bay Trilogy 1

Book 1 - Left For Dead

Book 2 - Circle of Lies

Book 3 - Truth Be Told

Morecambe Bay Trilogy 2

Book 4 - Trust Me Once

Book 5 - Fall From Grace

Book 6 - Bound By Blood

Morecambe Bay Trilogy 3

Book 7 - First To Die

Book 8 - Nothing To Lose

Book 9 - Last To Tell

Note: The Morecambe Bay trilogies are best read in the order shown above.

Don't Tell Meg Trilogy

Features DCI Kate Summers and Steven Terry.

Book 1 - Don't Tell Meg

Book 2 - The Murder Place

Book 3 - The Forgotten Children

Standalone Thrillers

One Last Chance

No More Secrets

So Many Lies

Two Years After

Friends Who Lie

Now You See Her

ABOUT THE AUTHOR

Hi, I'm Paul Teague, the author of the Morecambe Bay series and the Don't Tell Meg trilogy, as well as several other standalone psychological thrillers such as One Last Chance, Dead of Night and No More Secrets.

I'm a former broadcaster and journalist with the BBC, but I have also worked as a primary school teacher, a disc jockey, a shopkeeper, a waiter and a sales rep.

I've read thrillers all my life, starting with Enid Blyton's Famous Five series as a child, then graduating to James Hadley Chase, Harlan Coben, Linwood Barclay and Mark Edwards.

Let's get connected!
https://paulteague.net